fever

a Songbird novel

MELISSA PEARL

NOTE FROM THE AUTHOR

Music has always been an integral part of my life. My mother is an amazing singer and pianist, and I was raised with music always playing in the house. Sometimes I wonder if I could sing before I could talk. There is always a song flowing inside of me, no matter what I'm doing.

Being able to combine my passion for storytelling with my love for music has been a real treat. I know I'm going to relish writing every Songbird novel, because each one will have its own special soundtrack.

Fever is filled with jazz music. When I was in my early twenties, I met the man of my dreams. He loved jazz, and I'd never really given it a fair shot. It didn't take long to fall in love with both him and this genre of music.

"Cheek to Cheek" was the song we danced to at our wedding, and it will always hold a special place in my heart. Its placement in Ella and Cole's journey was very much intentional.

To me, music brings sunshine into my life. It makes the ordinary, extraordinary. Thank you for letting me share some of its magical qualities with you in this love story.

FEVER SOUNDTRACK

(Please note: The songs listed below are not always the original versions, but the ones I chose to listen to while constructing this book. Every song in the soundtrack is used in the book at some point.)

CHEEK TO CHEEK

THEY CAN'T TAKE THAT AWAY FROM ME

LET'S CALL THE WHOLE THING OFF

Performed by Louis Armstrong & Ella Fitzgerald

COME FLY WITH ME

Performed by Michael Buble

PUTTIN' ON THE RITZ

ANYTHING GOES

SOMEONE TO WATCH OVER ME

SUMMERTIME

Performed by Ella Fitzgerald

I WANNA KNOW YOUR NAME

Performed by The Intruders

STEPPIN' OUT WITH MY BABY

Performed by The Jumpin' Joz Band

FEVER

Performed by Peggy Lee

MACK THE KNIFE

Performed by Robbie Williams

STORMY WEAHTER

Performed by Sarah Vaughan

CRY ME A RIVER

Performed by Julie London

I JUST WANT TO MAKE LOVE TO YOU

Performed by Etta James

I WOULD WALK 500 MILES

Performed by The Proclaimers

For Ella Fitzgerald - the ultimate songbird.

ONE
ELLA

This was a mistake.

I was such an idiot!

Why did I agree to this?

My hands gripped the sides of my narrow airplane seat as the aircraft descended into O'Hare International Airport.

Morgan sat beside me, agitated and tutting; she hated being late. The flight from LAX had been delayed by over an hour, and it was pure torture for her. She looked at her watch again, clicking her tongue and holding in another sigh; I could tell by the way her cheeks were puffing.

"We should have left a week ago." She shook her head. "We've put so much pressure on ourselves now. Classes start tomorrow. You've

1

completely missed orientation, you'll only just make registration, and you still have to get your stuff sorted out." Her bottom lip protruded in an uncharacteristic pout. "Plus, I wanted to see Brad this afternoon."

She pressed her lips together, trying to hold back her myriad of complaints. I knew she felt bad, and I didn't want to rub her nose in it, but she was my friend and I had to say something.

"Staying for your little sister's eighteenth birthday party was the right thing to do. Jody's my best friend; I wasn't going to miss it."

Morgan conceded with an eye roll, her cheeks heating with color. "I know. I just wish the timing could have been better, that's all. Did she really have to celebrate on her *actual* birthday?"

I chuckled. "It's Jody, of course she did."

Morgan flicked me a dry look, her lips twitching.

I turned to peek out the window. My new home lay beneath me; the vast, sprawling city of Chicago. A city I'd never set foot in. Most people would probably have been giddy with excitement, but I just felt scared. Not that I'd ever admit it to Morgan or David, but I saw absolutely nothing wrong with a degree from Pasadena Community College, and I didn't know why I'd caved and agreed to apply to the University of Chicago! My boyfriend could be too persuasive sometimes. It was no surprise to anyone that he had his sights set on law school; he'd be an amazing lawyer.

I never expected to get into UChicago...and I certainly never expected to get awarded a partial scholarship. It was impossible to say no after that. So, after only one contented year at my little community college, I was shipping myself across the country to start a new life.

"It's only three years," I mumbled to myself.

It was an attempt at comfort, but it fell flat. It wasn't just three years. If David got his way, which he always seemed to, I might never make it back to LA. The idea should have been liberating. LA held a lot of bad memories for me, but it also held Jody and a life that brought with it a certain sense of security.

"Why am I doing this?" My head whipped back to Morgan.

Her tense face relaxed as she squeezed my arm. "Because you're an intelligent woman who deserves this chance. Just think of your parents."

That was the clincher. That's how they'd persuaded me to finally make the move. I hated them for bringing my parents into this, but David and Morgan were probably right.

"Besides, aren't you just so relieved to be out of your psychotic aunt's house? No more cats. No more anal reminders about how the towels should be hung just so. No more random rampages."

I cringed, picturing my aunt as she rained a flurry of words over me, telling me how useless I was and how I never seemed to pull my weight around the house.

I never asked to have you, Ella. The girls and I have had to sacrifice a lot to fit you into our lives. You should be grateful.

The girls! Ugh. She was more in love with those damn cats than any human beings. I still couldn't believe that woman was related to my mother; it didn't seem possible.

I squeezed my eyes shut, pressing my head against the seat back. "Come on, Morgan. You know I practically moved into your place when you left. I spent more nights sleeping in your old bed than my own. I only went back on the nights Aunt Fiona had a sudden surge of guilt and dragged me home, because *I was her responsibility.*"

Morgan chuckled at the fake voice I was using. "I know you're not going to miss that."

"I'll miss Jo-Jo, though."

Morgan squeezed my arm, making me look at her. "I know. It's just been the two of you—no David, no me—and you guys had a blast, but it's gonna be okay. You need to spread your wings, Ella. It's time for you to fly."

"I never asked to fly."

"Oh stop it." Morgan turned back to face the front, rubbing her ear as the plane drew closer to the ground.

Twenty minutes later, we landed with a soft bump and taxied toward the terminal. As soon as the wheels hit the tarmac, Morgan went into mother-mode. She'd been doing it since she was fourteen and had the whole deal down pat.

"Okay, so David said he'd pick us up. He better be there on time."

"You know he will."

"As soon as we get to the dorm, we'll drop our stuff and I'll quickly show you around the floor, but then I need to go find Brad. I hope that's okay. You don't mind unpacking on your own, do you?"

"I'll be okay. David said he'd give me a tour."

"Make sure he takes you past registration. You need to be sure of where all your classes are. I don't want you getting lost on the first day."

"I know. He'll definitely have to show me where my Monday classes are. I'm a bit nervous about that actually."

"You'll be fine. This is a big adventure, I know, but you can do this, sweets. You're gonna be awesome."

I forced a tight smile, my cheek muscles straining.

Morgan chuckled then broke into a grin. It was her big beaming one, so I knew she wasn't thinking about David as she leaned toward me with a little squeal. "I can't believe we're gonna be roomies! Having spent my first two years with Boring Doreen and then a hideous year with Slutbag Susanna, I am so excited that my senior year will be with my kick-ass bestie. I've missed you so much. Jody's had you all to herself, and now it's my turn."

I grinned; I couldn't help it. In spite of my trepidation, it was going to be cool living with Morgan again. We'd met when I was fifteen years old. Moving from Bellevue, Washington to Pasadena had been terrifying. As if my parents dying so suddenly hadn't been enough of a shock, I was then shipped off to live with Aunt Fiona. I wanted to die, literally, until I spotted a set of curious eyes watching me from her living room window. Without hesitation, she'd bounded out of the house and introduced herself.

Morgan Pritchett. She was two years my senior and her little sister was two years beneath me, but it didn't matter. By the end of my first month in Pasadena we'd become best friends and that status would never change. Mr. Pritchett called us the Terrible Trio, but it was always in jest. I could see tears glistening in his eyes as he hugged Morgan and me goodbye at the airport.

My eyes stung as I pictured him wrapping his arms around a sniffling Jody and waving us off at the gate.

Why did I leave them again?

The seatbelt sign dinged and the plane erupted with movement. Morgan was up and out of her seat in a second, her long body stretching high to lift our bags down. I stood awkwardly from my seat, trying not to stumble as I inched my way into the aisle. She passed my bag down to me, and I hefted it onto my shoulder, nearly getting pushed to the floor by the man in front of me. My face smashed into Morgan's chest.

"Sorry," I mumbled, pushing back and righting myself.

She chuckled and then put on her indignant face as she nudged the guy in front of me. "Watch it."

He turned to give her some snide remark, but his features changed when he took her in. Yes, Morgan was tall, like nearly five-foot-ten tall. Her sharp, brown gaze could pierce iron, and she had a way about her that screamed, "Don't mess with me. I will ruin you."

The guy backed off, finally having enough space to maneuver himself down the aisle. I grinned up at my friend before turning and shuffling after him.

As soon as we got off the plane, Morgan put on the speed. She always walked way too fast, in my opinion. Jody and I were often giggling about how we had to run to keep up with her. I puffed my way to the baggage carousel and waited in agitated silence for my big suitcase to trundle into view. It was so heavy, Morgan would have to help me lift it off. I clung to the luggage trolley as Morgan kept talking. I had started tuning out a few minutes ago, my mind growing fuzzy with fear. Everything within me wanted out. I wanted to go back. I wanted to drive Jody to school and then keep going on to PCC, just like I had every day last year.

Jitters sliced up my insides, attacking my core until I felt like crumbling. This was my first big move since I'd left Washington, and memories were coming thick and fast. Not actual memories, more like emotional memories. That feeling of the unknown swamping me, that pure vulnerability I'd endured as I walked out the arrivals gate to find my sour-faced aunt waiting for me. She was a pale, thin, ghostly lady, nothing like my fresh-faced mother. Unlike Aunt Fiona, my mom had been a woman of infinite joy; always laughing, her eyes sparkling like sapphires when she smiled. I missed her more than ever in times like these. If they'd still been alive, my dad would have been the one waiting for my suitcase while Mom fussed over me. As much as I loved Morgan, she was a poor substitute some days.

"Okay, let's go." She grunted, lifting my bag onto the trolley. I hadn't even seen it appear.

"Thanks." I forced yet another smile, trying to ward off the barrage of doubts that made me want to run back onto that plane and demand they fly me home.

Morgan clipped ahead of me in her shiny black shoes. She always looked so professional, her jeans pressed and pristine, her white shirt and navy jacket sitting perfectly. I glanced down at my rumpled checkered shirt and tried to tug the collar straight. Next to Morgan, I was like a kid. I think my forehead was in line with her chin, plus I looked young for my age. Aunt Fiona said I'd be grateful for that in the future, but for now, it was kind of annoying. Twice this summer, when I commented that I was going to be a sophomore, people assumed I meant high school.

Tucking a thick strand of my mouse-brown hair behind my ear, I walked quietly beside my large friend. She was scanning the crowd as we walked through the gate, her agitation quickly building.

It wasn't that she didn't like David; she just didn't love him. She never said this, but I could sense the hostile vibes between them sometimes. He didn't have to do much to spark her anger, but the problem was, David loved a good fight and he knew exactly how to needle my best friend. Thankfully we didn't get together until after Morgan left for her first year of college. If she'd been around, things might not have happened between David and me.

"Oh, he's here." Morgan sounded surprised as she pointed in his direction.

My eyes popped up and my insides swelled. He was grinning at me and had that adorable look in his brown eyes. I couldn't get enough of that dimple that scored his left cheek when he smiled. Letting go of the trolley with a little laugh, I raced toward him, loving the feel of his strong arms wrapping around my waist. I pressed my lips to his; they felt warm and familiar. I wanted to deepen the kiss, but he pulled back, aware we were in a public setting. He'd never been a huge fan of the whole PDA thing.

"Welcome to your new home." He touched his nose to mine and I bit my lip. I couldn't say anything. Instead, I closed my eyes and squeezed my arms a little tighter around his neck. I could have spent the rest of the day like that, but Morgan cleared her throat, so David let me go and took charge of the trolley.

"So, how was the flight?" He led us through the massive parking lot, pulling out his keys as we drew near to his black Honda Accord.

"It was pretty good. Sorry for the delay."

"No problem. I kept my entire day free." He winked at me before closing the trunk and opening the passenger door for me and then Morgan.

We hit the road and the trip passed by with amiable chatter. I quietly took in the surroundings as Morgan and David talked shop. They were both pretty focused on their studies, no one more so than David. Now in his junior year at UChicago, he had his sights set on Harvard Law. He'd get in for sure. He wanted to pass each year with an A+ average, which I thought was insane, but David was just that kind of guy; he liked being the best. People found his motivation and commitment inspiring.

"You're gonna love it, El. I just know it."

I nodded. His enthusiasm was starting to rub off, and a smile lit my features. A few minutes later we were pulling into Hyde Park and making our way through campus. It was a beautiful place, majestic even. Students milled around, sitting in clumps or walking across the grounds, excited chatter buzzing around them. I couldn't hear it from the car, but I could see it. I was one of them now — a UChicago student. I needed to start loving it as much as everyone else did.

Pulling in a breath, I reached for the handle and popped my door open. The sun was brilliant in the clear blue sky. It was the perfect day, and I had to enjoy this moment.

Looking across the roof of the car, I spotted David's elated grin. Maybe this would be okay.

So why could I not shake that damn question from circling my brain like a vulture?

Ella, what the hell are you doing here?

TWO

ELLA

"So, this is us." Morgan pushed the door open, revealing the room I'd seen on Skype many times. It was a pretty cool space, and I did feel lucky that Morgan had managed to secure this spot for me.

David walked ahead with my luggage, gliding through the small living area and dumping my suitcase on the bed. I stepped across the wooden floor and looked around the space. The long, flat couch took up most of the living area and was pointed at a small TV, resting on a wooden bookshelf crammed full of tatty novels. Morgan could power through a book on a good day, and that shelf was proof.

A chunky coffee table sat between the TV and the brown, tartan couch. Behind me was a small fridge next to a tidy desk with a lamp perched on the corner. To my right was my little room and opposite to that, across the living area, was Morgan's. We had a small double bed each, and next to my bed was an empty desk with a stool for a chair.

"I tend to study in the library. I try to think of this as a place where I can relax." Morgan crossed her arms, trying to assess me.

I nodded again and my smile actually grew to be genuine. I liked it. There was something comfortable about the space. Pictures of the Terrible Trio were plastered all over Morgan's door, bringing instant comfort. I chuckled as I stepped toward it and studied the different images.

"Feel free to put up whatever you like. Susanna cleaned out her room pretty good when she left, so make this place your home."

"I will, thanks."

"Come on, I'll show you where the bathrooms are." She pulled me out the door, calling to David that we'd be back in a minute. I bustled down the corridor and ducked out of the way of a freshman with a huge box in his hands; he looked as small and scared as I felt. I still wasn't sure if it was a good idea to have a mix of ages and genders on each floor, but Morgan seemed to like it, and I had to trust my friend.

Morgan pushed the bathroom door open. "So, the busiest shower times are always in the morning and usually about six 'til seven at night. So if you don't want to be waiting in line for a shower, come either really early or late." She flung back a shower curtain, showing me the clean stall with three little hooks lined up across the steel frame. I looked around the cubicle and swallowed. It felt weird to know I'd be naked in the same room as other people with a flimsy shower curtain as my only form of protection. I was used to showering behind a locked door.

I leaned my head against the frame and looked at Morgan.

"It's gonna be okay. You'll get used to it."

I opened my mouth to say it, but she cut me off.

"You're here because this is a great opportunity for you."

"What if it all falls apart?"

"It won't, but if it does, we'll pick up the pieces and move on. You can do this, Ella Bella."

I sniffed out a chuckle and wrapped my arms around her waist. She rested her chin on my head and squeezed back.

David was waiting on the edge of my bed with his arms folded across his chest. His head whipped in my direction as I stepped into the room, and it was hard to miss the desire in his gaze.

Morgan cleared her throat and grabbed for her purse. "I'm gonna unpack later. I want to see Brad. Text me if you need anything."

The door clicked shut behind her and I felt a little bereft, but then David's arms were around me and the feeling dissipated, replaced with hot kisses. He cupped the back of my head, his other arm squeezing me close against him. I kissed back, enjoying the feel of his strong body, but I just couldn't get into it.

I pulled back, kissing his neck to soften the move. "I want to make sure my registration is all set, plus I need a tour of this place. I want to get my bearings before tomorrow."

"You can get your bearings later." He nuzzled my neck, his hands trailing up my ribcage.

"David..." I started to say, but he silenced me with a kiss. He leaned me back, his mouth fastened to mine, and I knew I wouldn't be able to resist him.

He opened his eyes and gazed down at me. "You really want to wait?" he asked, his breathing heavy.

"No," I said, trailing my finger down his cheek. "But I'm nervous and if I don't go and register soon, I'm gonna be a complete wreck. I need to know exactly where I have to go tomorrow. You know I get antsy with new stuff." I held back just how much I was truly freaking out. I didn't want to make him feel bad. It was, after all, his drive that got me over here.

His gaze softened with that tender look I loved. "You have nothing to worry about, baby. I've already ordered all your books and the stuff you'll need. The only thing left to do is to check you in and then show you around. This place is amazing and you're gonna love it. Trust me." He pecked my cheek. "Come on, grab your stuff and we'll get going."

I fished my purse out of my large bag and threw my wallet and phone into the front pocket. Running my hands through my hair, I tried to brush out the knots and straighten up.

"You look great." With a grin, he reached for my hand. I took it like a lifeline, remembering the first time he'd smiled at me that way.

It was the second month of my junior year at Pasadena High. Morgan had left for college, leaving me feeling a little lost and sending Jody on a rebellious spiral. It's like Jo-Jo had been waiting for her big sister to get out of town so she could let loose; the fact it coincided with her starting high school didn't really help, either. I was struggling to rein in the wild freshman and feeling hopeless. David saw my desolate form sitting alone in the cafeteria watching Jody flirt mindlessly with Craig Winston, the school womanizer. He'd sat down in front of me, cutting off my view and giving me that smile.

"*Want to talk about it?*"

"*I don't even know your name.*" I blushed, looking to the table. I actually did know his name, but we'd never been formally introduced. There was no way I'd ever have the courage to approach him. He was way handsome and he might not have been the star quarterback, but he was senior class president and really popular. He was so out of my league it wasn't even funny.

"*David Kellerman.*" He chuckled and held out his hand. "*And you're Ella Simmons.*"

I took his hand, a light frown denting my forehead. He knew my name? How was that even possible?

"*I hope you don't mind.*" He leaned across the table. "*I kinda asked around.*" Scratching the top of his head, his cheeks lit with a soft blush before that dimple of his appeared. "*I've been wanting to talk to you for weeks, but I didn't want to scare you off or anything.*"

My mouth dropped open. He'd noticed me? Little, mousy Ella Simmons? I glanced over my shoulder, wondering if this was some kind of prank, but I knew it couldn't be. David Kellerman wasn't that kind of guy. He was nice, intelligent, sweet...and he wanted to talk to ME.

I looked back into his soft, brown eyes and smiled. I couldn't hold it for long, my traitorous teeth pinching my bottom lip. I looked back to the table. My cheeks felt like they were about to combust, they were so hot.

David tapped his knuckles lightly on the table. "*I just saw you sitting over here looking kind of sad and, well...I thought you could use a friend.*" He glanced over his shoulder, catching a glimpse of Jody throwing back her perfect blonde curls and laughing like a hyena. "*That's Morgan Pritchett's little sister, right?*"

I nodded.

"*You guys are pretty tight.*"

"*Yeah, like family,*" I whispered.

He shot me a glum smile of sympathy. "*So, do you*

want to talk about it?"

And that had been the start. David had pulled me into his life, providing me with all the safety I craved. He even helped me get Jody straightened out, and my junior year at Pasadena High had ended up being the best in my life.

"You're going to love this place." David pulled me from my memories as we walked out into the sunshine. "There's so much cool stuff here and Chicago is such a great city. But this campus right here." He pointed at the ground. "This is the coolest place on earth."

His enthusiasm didn't wane, not for a micro-second. After registration, we collected my books from the University bookstore and he dragged me from one end of the campus to the other, showing me exactly where all my classes were...as well as his. By the end, my mind was a jumble of directions, and I was freaking out that I'd end up getting lost in the morning.

"You know, my first class isn't until nine, so I have time to walk you to Comparative Literature if you like."

I swallowed and nodded yet again. My neck muscles were going to be spasming by the end of the day.

"Hey, Ella, it's gonna be okay. I'll take care of you here, I promise."

"Thanks." I squeezed his hand as we walked back into the dorm and made our way to the third floor. I was trying to remember which corridor to take when he pulled me to a stop and leaned against door 309.

"This is me." His dimple appeared as he slid the heavy book bag off his shoulder. "And you're just down the hall and to the right." I looked in the direction of his pointing finger and nodded.

Right. Remember right.

He chuckled. "I know your sense of direction sucks, so just remember 309 and you'll be fine."

I grinned. "309 and I'll be fine. Got it. And I'm 315, right?"

"Right."

"Okay." I nodded, breathing out and holding his arms as he pulled me against him.

"But remember, you can always bunk here anytime you like." He wiggled his eyebrows.

I snickered and pressed my forehead against his shoulder. I swallowed, feeling bad for what I was about to say, but my nerves were strung too tight. There was no way I could get naked with him right now and enjoy it. "If it's okay, I might spend my first night getting my own space organized, but thanks for the offer."

He made a little whine in his throat, sounding like a puppy dog. "Don't make me wait too long. I've missed you."

I chuckled. "You just saw me two weeks ago."

"I know." He kissed the top of my head. "But even that's been too long."

I lifted my head and looked up at him. "Hey, I'm here now...for the rest of the year. We'll have plenty of time together."

His eyes sparkled. "Yes, we will."

Man, I couldn't get enough of that grin. Rising to my tiptoes, I planted a kiss on his lips and then moved away from him. I hefted the bag onto my shoulder.

"Here, let me at least carry those for you."

"No, I'll be okay." I forced a sunny grin. His eyes narrowed, but I put on a brave face, pretending the weight cutting into my shoulder was no big deal as I walked away.

I could tell he was watching me. I tried really hard not to look back but had to make sure, pausing at the end of the hallway and pointing where I thought I should go. He nodded and I shuffled that way before he could laugh at me anymore. I really wished I had a better sense of direction.

I reached my room and found it empty. Morgan was obviously still catching up with Brad. They'd only seen each other for a few days over the summer, and I could imagine exactly how they were making up for lost time. I was relieved they were doing it at his place and not ours.

Walking through the quiet apartment, I perched my butt on the edge of my bed. The book bag thumped to the floor, and I wrapped my arms around myself.

"It will be okay, you know." Saying the words aloud didn't really help.

Would it be okay?

I hated that I felt so insecure. David and Morgan were both here. I was surrounded by people who loved me; I should be excited. Their plans for me made sense...they were great! So why was I so damn scared?

Morgan had been right; I needed to spread my wings, fly a little. David did the right thing in encouraging me here. My dreams were basically non-existent compared to his. His vision for our future was so massive, I didn't really need any dreams of my own. He was good for me. He said he'd take care of me and I believed him.

I just never thought that following in his footsteps could make me feel so lost.

THREE

COLE

"You lose! Woohoo!"

I watched Frankie prance around like an idiot, a pool cue in one hand while the other punched the air. I understood the fourteen-year-old's elation. Beating Malachi Quigg at pool was damn near impossible. I'd been trying for years and only managed it a couple of times.

Throwing the damp cloth from my hand to the counter top, I continued wiping down the bar while Nina bustled in from the kitchen with an empty tray to collect up the remaining glasses from the pub tables.

I grinned as she hummed her way around the room. It had been a busy one tonight; the sturdy, wooden tables filled with people enjoying plates piled high with food and mugs nearly overflowing with thick, Irish ale.

People came from all over Chicago to hang out at Quigg's. It was a friendly joint that Malachi and Nina had started up on their meager savings. They wanted it to be a place that everyone felt comfortable in. Sunday lunches saw families with young kids shuffling in the door while Friday nights often brought in a fresh haul of college students. They were stubbornly strict on checking IDs from anyone who looked mildly underage, and alcohol was served accordingly. I had been given very clear instructions when I first started working behind the bar. It'd been drummed into me so hard, I could practically recite the rules in my sleep.

I finished wiping down the polished wood until it gleamed and then pulled the dishtowel off my shoulder to dry off any remaining watermarks. Nina dumped the tray onto the edge of the bar and I took it off her, walking back into the kitchen and leaving it by the sink for Declan to deal with in the morning.

Stepping back into the room, I spotted Nina, her freckled face scrunched tightly in disgust.

"I'm guessing this is yours."

She held up the small, white napkin with a phone number scribbled across the center.

"Ah, that's right. Candace." I took it from her, folding it in half and slipping it into my back pocket.

Nina slumped onto the bar with a groan, her red hair splaying over the wood.

"Are you even going to call her?"

I made my grin extra-wide as she looked at me with that droll expression of hers. "Of course I'm gonna call her."

"Yeah, for a booty call!" Frankie jumped up onto the stool beside his foster mother and chortled.

"Frankie," she scolded and turned back to me with a glare. "See the example you're setting right now?"

"Oh come on, Nina." Frankie rolled his eyes. "You don't think I'm good with the ladies?"

Nina squashed her grin between tight lips and turned back to the boy. "You're fourteen years old. Let me assure you, you have a very long way to go before you score yourself a decent lady. Now back to bed, mister. You've got school tomorrow."

"Malachi said we could play another game."

Nina's green eyes rounded. "It's getting close to midnight, and Malachi is not allowed to say those things to you without my permission. Now, bed. Sleep. Grow!"

With an impish grin, Frankie slid from his stool and bustled past his foster father. Malachi scruffed the boy's hair as he walked past, putting on an innocent face. "What's he doing up then?"

Nina gave him a hard glare before turning to check the pub doors were locked. "That kid does not understand the concept of sleep, and you letting him play pool after closing does not help, Mal. He should have been in bed hours ago. If the place hadn't been so busy tonight, I would have been up there with him. I feel bad when I can't look after him properly." She turned back with a frown.

Her soft heart was her undoing...and the reason every foster child who had ever been in her care fell madly in love with her.

"You remember what I was like when you first got me. Sleep's hard for a foster kid." I threw the dishtowel back over my shoulder. "Besides, trying to beat Malachi at pool is probably keeping that kid from running away."

Nina gave me a soft smile. "I just hope the state will let us keep him. I feel like we can really make a difference with this one. If we're lucky enough, he'll turn out as brilliant as you."

I grinned as she patted my arm. She'd never be my real mother, but she certainly treated me like her son, as she did every boy who'd been dropped off at her door. "Frankie's a good kid. He'll be fine."

"Yeah, as long as we can keep him away from that psycho mother of his." Malachi's eyes bulged, his Irish accent growing thick with the late hour.

"Mal," Nina chided.

"What? I only speak the truth."

"I know." Nina looked toward the door that led up to the three-bedroom apartment above us. "But he doesn't need to hear us talking that way. A boy will always love his mother, no matter how messed up she is."

Nina picked at the counter, and I couldn't help leaning over the bar and kissing her cheek. "You're the world's best mother, Nina. He'll fall in love with you, too. In fact, I think he already has a little bit."

"Well, it's impossible not to, Boy-o. Look at the woman, she's the most beautiful creature on this earth."

Nina blushed and rolled her eyes as her husband captured her from behind, wrapping his arms around her waist and nuzzling her neck. "Malachi, stop it."

Finally relenting, he grabbed the broom from the closet and started sweeping up the floor, giving her neck a raspberry as he walked past her. I chuckled with Malachi as Nina yelped and slapped him on the back. The three of us continued packing up, each knowing our jobs without having to say a thing. I'd started working weekend shifts here when I was sixteen. Five years later, I felt like a pro and couldn't wait to start doing this on my own.

"Speaking of falling in love." Nina sat down at the bar, her perfect nose crinkling.

"When were we speaking of falling in love?" I tipped my head. She always did this to me.

"We are now." She slapped the counter and I bit back my smile, reaching for a short glass and popping the cap off her favorite bottle of whisky.

She took the glass with a little smile and raised it in the air before taking a delicate sip. "When are you going to stop collecting all these random phone numbers and actually start dating a girl, Cole Reynolds?"

"I date."

"No, you don't; you charm, you swoon, you sleep with and then you don't commit."

"Hey, I don't sleep around like that, okay?"

"You're telling me you haven't had sex with any of the girls who practically throw their phone numbers at you?"

"That's not what I'm saying either."

"Then what are you saying?" Malachi slipped into the seat beside his wife and tapped the counter.

With a scowl, I pulled up another glass and slapped it down. "You're making me sound like a jerk."

Malachi chuckled while I filled his glass a third of the way with the amber liquid.

Nina took another sip and placed her glass down with a grin. "You're not a jerk, Cole. You are a gorgeous guy that girls fall all over themselves to get to. I'm just wondering when one of them will actually get under your skin."

"I don't know if one ever will." I shrugged, hating this conversation. I had plans, and a committed relationship was certainly not on the agenda.

"What? You don't want to fall in love and have babies?" Malachi looked incredulous. "You'd be such a great father."

"I'm twenty-one. Are we really having the parenthood discussion right now?" I put the bottle away and turned back to face them.

"We're not saying we want you to be a father now, we're just wondering if it's a dream you have for the future." Nina's eyes sparkled.

I pressed my arms against the bar and got in her face. "You know the only dream I have for my future is to own a pub like this. I want to give indie bands a place to play, and people a place to dance, sing, and have a little fun in. Your gig here is awesome and I want to do it too. I got one year left until I graduate, and then I can focus all my attention on making it happen."

"You gonna be my competition, Boy-o?"

I chuckled. "You know I'm gonna set it up on the South Side. I could cater to all the college students. There's nothing like that for us near campus. It'd become like a student watering hole."

"An alcohol-free one?" Malachi's bushy eyebrows rose.

I looked him straight in the eye. Blue on blue. It was always the best way to have a serious conversation with him. "If I need it to be, I will. Students will come for the music and the cheap food, not the booze."

"Highly unlikely," Malachi scoffed.

"I love your dream." Nina ran her hand over my messy curls. "You remind me so much of what Malachi was like when I first met him. He had such grand plans."

I shifted away from her, my back cramping from leaning forward so far. I crossed my arms over my chest and nodded. "See? And he made them happen."

"No." Nina shook her head. "*We* made them happen. Together." She caught Malachi's eye, and they shared one of those moments, both their expressions turning mushy.

"I can tell you, boy, it's a lot more fun that way," Malachi stated. "You have someone to stress with. Someone to celebrate with...and then of course there's the sex-breaks." His cheeky grin accompanied Nina's gasp. "Oh you know you loved it, you little minx."

"Malachi Quigg, if you ever want sex again you will stop talking right now." She gave him a stern frown, hampered with giggles, before draining her glass and passing it back to me.

I took it with a laugh, holding out my free hand for Malachi's. "I know one day I'll probably fall in love with a very nice woman and we'll be happy together, but I just can't imagine wanting that more than my plans right now. I don't know if everyone finds their soul mate like you two did. I think there are many contented, happy couples in the world, and I think it's possible to love lots of different people."

Nina's nose wrinkled.

"Come on." I spread my arms wide. "I kind of like the idea that if my spouse died, I'd have the chance to fall in love with someone else."

"Okay, fair point. You might never find your soul mate, but you can't dance with a bar, and a bar will never wrap its arms around you and make you feel more loved than anything else ever can."

Nina's green eyes bored into me and I had to concede. You could dance on a bar, but it certainly wouldn't be kissing you goodnight.

"I'm not going to stop praying for you, kid. I want you to find that girl. I want you to build your dreams together."

"You do that, Nina." I forced a small grin.

"Oh I will." Jumping down from the bar, she blew me a kiss and headed for the stairwell. "I'm gonna go check on Frankie. You have a good day tomorrow."

"Yeah, I better get going. My first class is at eight-thirty."

She stopped at the door, pride shining in her expression. "Good luck. And say hi to David for us. Tell him he has to stop by for a meal."

"Will do." I waved them goodbye and slipped out the back, hearing Malachi lock the door behind me. The evening air felt fresh on my face. Man, I loved this time of night. The city still had a buzz to it, but it was softer and less intrusive.

I caught a cab easily and was soon handing over my cash and taking the stairs two at a time to my dorm room.

I couldn't stop thinking about what Nina had said. The whole falling-in-love thing irked me. I didn't want to need it. I didn't want to see how happy my foster parents were together and then yearn for the same thing. I'd been on my own since I was ten, fending for myself; I was used to it. But Nina and Malachi had really picked away at my barriers. When I'd first arrived on their doorstep, I was a messed-up fourteen-year-old, and the first thing to really break through my stone wall was the loving way they treated each other. The way they laughed together, danced together, sang around each other as they cleaned up the bar. Or the way Malachi would sometimes just sit there, watching his wife. She was oblivious to his gaze in spite of the love emanating from it. I couldn't help wondering what that felt like.

I opened the door quietly, knowing David would already be asleep. He'd moved in with me my sophomore year and swiftly become my best friend on campus. He was a good guy—intelligent, funny, easy to be around—but he was also super-studious and got a little pissy with my work hours sometimes.

I crept past his door, wondering if his girlfriend was nestled up beside him. I knew she was arriving today, and I knew he couldn't wait to introduce me. For the life of me, I could not remember her name. Sneaking over to the bulletin board above his desk, I shifted aside the class schedules and study plans, finally unearthing a picture of her.

She had a broad, yet tentative, smile. She was tucked under David's arm as he beamed at the camera. Maybe having a long-term girlfriend was a good thing. I mean, these guys had made it work long-distance for two years; that had to say something about how awesome it could be. I dropped the papers, covering up the image, and shook my head. I just didn't see the point of continually hanging out with a girl who didn't set my insides on fire. I wanted to be inspired. There was no way I wanted to settle.

Sure, I didn't believe in soul mates, but I also didn't believe in being with someone who bored me to tears. What was the point? I'd rather be single.

Dragging my tired ass toward the bed, I knew I should probably have been collecting my stuff and taking a shower, but I couldn't be bothered. I squinted at my watch, setting the alarm for 5:30 a.m.; I'd beat the early rush that way and still have plenty of time to get my stuff organized for the week ahead.

I kicked off my shoes, punched the pillow beneath my head and shuffled around until I was comfy. A slow smile spread across my lips. Tomorrow was the first day of my senior year. In less than a year, I'd be a free agent and then I could really start making my dreams come true.

FOUR
ELLA

I didn't need an alarm to wake me; I had barely slept and by five, I'd given up. My dreams had been stuffed full of worries, my mind racing from one weird scenario to another. Nerves were doing my stomach in, making me feel nauseated, and I felt immature and stupid for being such a wreck. I'd already done a year in college for crying out loud; what the hell was my problem?

I guess I was just nervous about screwing up. What if I got lost? What if I missed a class? What if...what if...what if.

"Arrggggh! Stop it, Ella! You're gonna drive yourself insane," I whispered into the darkness.

Flinging back the covers, I checked my watch again.

5:28 a.m.

I couldn't lay in bed for one more second. Turning on my lamp, I squinted against the sudden brightness and shuffled about the room. I heard Morgan creep in sometime around ten last night but didn't get up to say hi. I didn't want to talk, and Morgan always siphoned stuff out of me. She had the uncanny ability to get the truth out of people. She should be training to be an interrogator, not spending her days studying some vague business degree that gave her plenty of options and no real direction.

Pulling on my sweats, I grabbed my fluffy, yellow towel and my toiletries. This early, I should definitely miss the shower rush.

I was right.

A smile stretched my lips wide as I flicked on the lights and walked past empty stall after empty stall. I stopped at the very end one, arranging my stuff and feeling better by the second. I loved showers; they always calmed me. It was my own private time away from the world. It was weird not having a locked door, and it was weird to think that someone might walk in at any moment, but for now, I felt safe.

Flicking on the shower, I let the water heat while I undressed, a tune already working its way from my voice box. I only ever sang in private, and the shower head was my ultimate microphone. I had toyed with the idea of singing in public once; not for the spotlight or anything, just for the opportunity to sing. I really did love it, but I couldn't imagine ever having the guts to go through with it. Singing in front of an audience? Kill me now! I'd be so petrified.

Besides, every note I sang was peppered with an eerie feeling of melancholy. It wasn't enough for me to stop singing, but it was enough for me to never want to show it to a crowd. No, I sang for me and me alone. Anyway, the kind of music that really set my soul on fire was hardly considered cool. Jody and Morgan were the only ones who knew about my love affair with jazz music, and if I had any say in it, they'd be the only ones who ever did.

A memory skittered through my brain and I winced.

"What are you doing?" David appeared behind me, pressing his hand against the wall and boxing me in as I read the Pasadena High Jazz Club audition notice. They were looking for a couple of backup singers.

I shrugged, trying to ignore his derogatory tone. "I was just looking."

"Jazz Club?" David chuckled. "How would you stand it? I hate that kind of music. It's decades old."

"I know, but music can be timeless."

"Not this music."

I glanced around in time to see his face. Pressing my lips together, I tried not to let his words rile me. As if the annoying techno beats he always blasted in his car would ever stand the test of time.

"You're not seriously thinking of auditioning, are you? I didn't even know you could sing."

"I don't, really. I just muck around with Jody sometimes." I shook my head, stepping back from the school bulletin board, inspired with a quick lie. "Actually, I was thinking of Jody, not me. You know how amazing her voice is. She'll sing anything."

"Yeah." David rolled his eyes. "I know."

"Hey." I lightly tugged his shirt. "She's good."

"Oh yeah, she's amazing. Sorry, I wasn't trying to be mean."

"I know." I forced a grin.

"But, don't you think she's involved in enough stuff? I mean, now that she's over her wild rampage, she's

*actually busy with Glee Club and choir and dance. Do
we really want her to get involved in yet another thing
we'll have to go and watch?"*

*My nose wrinkled before I could stop it. "You don't
like watching Jody perform?"*

*"Oh no, of course I do." His dimple appeared, but the
way he ran his hand through his hair told me he was
hedging. "I just..." He cleared his throat, pointing back
at the board. "I just don't want to have to sit through
jazz as well. Please, could you just not show her this
one...for me?"*

*His soft gaze was on full-beam and I always found it
impossible to resist. We'd been dating nearly six
months, and the desire to please him was just as strong
as the day he first asked me out. I didn't always
understand the power he seemed to have over me, but I
knew I never wanted to lose him, and so I nodded and
took his hand, turning away from the audition notice
and vowing never to give away my secret.*

My skeleton remained locked up tight in a
shower cubicle and I was happy to keep it there. It
was probably the reason why I always had such
long showers. Aunt Fiona used to tell me off for
using up all the hot water. She'd bang on the door,
interrupting me mid-verse, and tell me to hurry up.
Wretched woman. She never knew how to have
any fun. Her showers lasted a minute, tops. In,
soap, wash, out. She had no concept of how
luxurious a shower could really be.

I danced my fingers under the hot spray and
sighed.

Heaven.

I stepped into the hot oasis and stretched my
neck back, letting the water run down my front,
heating me, soaking into my skin. I closed my eyes.

"Heaven," I sang the word in a whisper. "I'm in
heaven."

My voice grew stronger as I sang through the first verse of "Cheek to Cheek." Louis Armstrong and Ella Fitzgerald sang my favorite version of the song. I was so in love with those two, probably because my mother was a jazz/swing freak. Frank Sinatra, Nat King Cole, Louis Armstrong...they were always filling our house with music. But Ella, she was my mom's favorite, and she'd quickly become mine. The woman had a voice like an angel...the supreme songbird, Mom used to say.

I ended the verse strong on the high note and was about to dip low for the last line when a deep, masculine voice joined me from the other side of the wall.

"When we're out together dancing cheek to cheek."

My breath hitched, my heart rate tripling. Man, that was a sexy voice. My insides flooded with heat and it wasn't because of the shower. I bit my lip, wondering how to respond. My mind flashed with images of a naked man beneath his own shower head. What did he look like? If the person matched the voice, he must be built like a Greek god. My insides coiled tight as I touched the tiles in front of me.

I'd never had such a physical reaction to someone's voice before. I mean, yeah, David was sexy in his own way, but whoever was on the other side of the wall was making my knees weak.

The man chuckled, a low, gruff sound from his throat...at least I thought it was a chuckle. It was kind of hard to hear through the wall, but then he started singing again and I heard the smooth sound with crystal clarity. "Oh, I'd love to climb a mountain and to reach the highest peak."

He paused.

Waiting.

For me.

Pressing my lips together, I blinked a couple of times and then grinned.

FIVE
COLE

My alarm jolted me awake, piercing my sleep like a sword through the brain. I reached for my watch and scrambled to turn it off, tempted to roll over and forget it ever started beeping. My eyes were just closing when I let out a groggy groan.

"Get your ass up, Cole," I mumbled, forcing my body out of bed.

Scrubbing a hand over my face, I rubbed the back of my neck, trying to encourage my fuzzy brain into operation. The best thing to wake me up would be a shower. I grabbed my stuff and stumbled out the door.

The corridors were empty, and I liked it that way. I threw back the men's bathroom door and hit the lights, heading for the end stall. It was the only one I used. Not sure why, just a habit I didn't want to kick.

Flinging back the curtain, I flicked on the spray and quickly undressed. The water grew hot quickly, which was awesome. I wished the spray was a little stronger. I liked those showers that pelted your flesh, hot and hard, but getting that in these dorms was nothing but a pipedream. I'd have to swing by Nina and Mal's one night for a taste of luxury. I found more and more excuses to shower at their place since their new bathroom had been installed. Go for a meal; take a shower.

I grinned as I pictured Nina's eye roll. She told me I was ridiculous, but she didn't understand the true luxury of a shower. I stepped under the spray, throwing my head under right away and reaching for the shampoo. I was just lathering up when I heard it.

The voice of an angel.

It was soft at first, making me second-guess myself, but it grew with strength, and I had soon picked up the lines of "Cheek to Cheek." Hmmmm, a jazz fan.

Nina was a jazz freak. Frank Sinatra, Louis Armstrong, Cole Porter, she had it all, but nothing got her smiling like Ella Fitzgerald; she played that stuff all the time. As a teen, I used to moan and try for something else, but the music grew on me and the lyrics were permanently embedded in my brain.

This chick singing on the other side of the wall had an Ella essence about her. It was a beautiful sound and I found myself mesmerized, shampoo suds running down the back of my neck, unnoticed.

Her sweet voice paused to take a breath, and I couldn't help myself. I sung the next line loud and clear.

"When we're out together, dancing cheek to cheek."

There was an abrupt pause. I grinned. I must have scared her. Licking my lips, I sang the next line and stopped. It was her turn. Would she join me? I hoped so. I wanted to hear that voice again. It was so sweet and pure. It did something to me. My insides stirred with longing as I pictured what she might look like. I bet she was petite. She sounded small. Small and sweet.

I felt like I was trying to coax a timid sparrow into my hand and was about to open my mouth to sing the next line when she sang it for me.

"But it doesn't thrill me half as much as dancing cheek to cheek." She put a slight spin on the melody that I loved. I smiled so wide my cheeks hurt. She kept going with the song and I joined her again. Her volume increased as she got into it. She even harmonized with me on the last chorus. I had to say, for someone who never sings in public, I felt like I sounded pretty damn good alongside her.

She had to be a music major or something. Surely. With a voice that sweet.

The song came to a finish, and I almost felt bereft. I didn't want it to end, so before thought could stop me, I started singing my favorite song from that era: "They Can't Take That Away From Me." I liked the Frank Sinatra version best, although Robbie Williams had done a pretty good job of it, too.

I heard her giggling as I finished the first line, and her voice immediately followed, sweetly floating over the notes with perfect pitch. I spun as I sang, rinsing off my hair and throwing my voice to the sky. It was easy to forget the world existed for a moment. This girl and me were the only people on the planet, just singing away to each other...a perfect moment.

We held the last note, both chuckling as we caught our breath. I was about to launch into another number when I heard the bathroom door squeak. I flicked off the spray and listened to shuffling feet down the end of the line. Moments later the shower was flicked on, ending my heavenly morning and bringing me back to reality.

Touching the tiles on the wall, I called out. "Hey, are you still there?"

"Yes." Her reply was soft, tentative.

"You...you sound like an angel. I swear, a voice straight from heaven." I heard a muffled titter and could picture her blushing up a storm. I needed to see her. I wanted to know the color of her eyes, see what type of mouth that melody flowed from. "I'll meet you outside."

She didn't say anything, so I took it as a yes. Grabbing my towel, I dried off in record time and threw on my clothes, using my fingers as a comb. It didn't make that much of a difference; my curls were pretty hard to control, which was why I liked to keep my hair on the shorter side. I wondered if she liked curly hair.

I rolled my eyes and laughed at myself. Since when had I ever cared what a girl thought of me? This was insane!

My insides were giddy with excitement as I raced into the hall and whipped around the corner to the girl's bathroom door. I didn't see anyone lingering outside and figured she was still getting dressed. Man, I couldn't wait to see what she looked like. Images built themselves inside my mind, being tossed aside for newer versions as I leaned against the wall and waited. I didn't want to look like a stalker or anything, so I tried for casual, crossing my legs at the ankles and leaning my head back against the wall.

It felt like it took forever, but finally the

bathroom door crept open and a spindly girl with long, blonde hair stepped out of the room. Her pale-brown eyes caught me gazing at her and she smiled.

"Hey." I stepped forward, probably looking like a dope. I didn't know what my face was doing, but I felt like my smile was really goofy.

She blushed, looking shy as she tucked a strand of hair behind her ear. "Hi." Her brow flickered, but then her lips spread with a smile.

"I'm Cole." I held out my hand, wanting to feel her, experience even the smallest touch of my shower bird.

She took my hand, her long fingers gently squeezing mine. She still looked slightly confused by my forthright introduction, but surely she knew I wanted to talk to her. That moment we'd just shared wasn't only magical for me, was it?

I cleared my throat. "Can I walk you to your room?"

She glanced down the hall and then back to me, her shoulders finally lifting in a shrug. "Sure, I guess so."

She turned and I followed her, unable to keep looking across at her. She was pretty tall. Nothing like my six-one, but she wouldn't have to tiptoe to kiss me. I guess I was wrong about the petite thing, but she was pretty. I liked her lopsided grin and the way she kept glancing at me and then blushing.

"So what's your name then, or are you gonna make me guess?"

She giggled, turning left down the corridor. "Caroline."

I played the name in my head, liking the sound of it. "Caroline. It's nice to meet you."

SIX

ELLA

I stood in the shower, clutching the towel to my chest. I'd turned the spray off the second he asked to meet me outside and then I'd frozen. Meet him? I couldn't do that.

It didn't matter that his voice was the sexiest thing I'd ever heard. Actually it totally mattered! That's exactly why I couldn't meet him outside. I had a boyfriend!

My body was still zinging from the sound of his voice floating over the shower wall. It was luscious and I wanted to know where that sound came from...probably a broad chest. His voice was rich and deep. I imagined the way his lips moved as they sang the lyrics and couldn't help wondering what they felt like...tasted like. Heat shot through my core, settling between my legs.

Squeezing my eyes shut, I lightly tapped my head against the tiles. This was ridiculous.

I. Had. A. Boyfriend.

I took my time and slowly dried off. As I lifted my foot to dry down my leg, I noticed there was another shower running. Oh crap, I hadn't even heard her come in. Had she heard me singing? How embarrassing.

I wanted to die.

"You sound like an angel... a voice straight from heaven."

My insides turned to mush as I relived the words. Shower man thought I sounded like an angel. Someone had heard me sing jazz of all things and hadn't ridiculed me or laughed in my face. Instead, he'd given me the best compliment I could ever get. A memory from long ago, buried beneath the rubble of hurt and anguish began to claw its way to the surface.

I bit my lip, my breaths coming out shaky. I squeezed my eyes shut, forcing my insides to settle. They managed to get down to a tremor as I held the towel in place with my chin and scurried to get dressed. Fiddling with the clasp of my bra, I clipped it into place before slipping my panties on. I tried not to let my wet feet touch the sides, but they inevitably did and I had to wiggle to get the damp fabric to sit right. Wrestling to get my sweats on without them touching the steamy tiles at my feet, I heard the shower flick off. I held my breath, hoping she wouldn't hear me.

Hanging my towel on the hook, I reached for my shirt. I was just slipping my flip-flops on when I heard the other girl fling the curtain back. Man she was fast.

If I waited a few more seconds, Miss Speedy would probably end up leaving before me, or if we both walked out together, maybe my shower man wouldn't feel confident approaching us. It was the safer option, and so I slowly extracted my brush and began running it through my hair, listening for the girl's departure. It didn't take long.

I peeked my head out of the stall and watched the tall, blonde girl leaving. It almost looked like Morgan, but her hair was too straight and long to be my friend's. She was also way skinnier than Morgan. Straight as an arrow.

I cleared my throat, once again hating my timidity. Why was I always such a chicken?

Taking my time, I left the shower and inched my way to the door. It flew open before I could reach for it. Two girls stepped into the room, chatting like magpies. I moved out of their way and waited until they were in their stalls before creeping out the door.

I looked up as I stepped into the corridor and actually felt disappointed to see that no guy was lingering in the hallway. Mystery man must have given up, which was a good thing.

So why did I feel so disappointed? Wouldn't it have been better to meet him and just explain I was already in a committed relationship?

For all I knew, he only wanted to see me out of curiosity anyway.

I couldn't help glancing down the corridor both ways. The hallways were much busier now, people rising to get ready for their classes. My chances of picking him out were now zero, but I couldn't help trying anyway.

"You're not lost already are you, baby?"

David's hand slid down my back, making me jump. I spun to face him, forcing a laugh that sounded breathy and stupid.

"No, I'm not lost." I pointed behind him. "That way, right?"

He looked over his shoulder. "You got it."

I grinned at him, loving that dimple and feeling secure now that he stood before me. Yeah, it was better that shower guy and I never met. It would just complicate everything. I didn't need complications. I was already worried enough about today.

"So, should I meet you in the cafeteria for breakfast?" I ran my hand down the towel flung over his shoulder.

"Yeah." He kissed my lips quickly. "I can only manage a quick bite though. Some of my study group from last year wants to get together this morning to go over our class schedules."

"Oh, so you can't walk me to Comparative Lit anymore?"

He winced. "No, sorry, but you'll be all right, won't you?"

I swallowed. "Yeah, of course. Uh-huh." I nodded.

David's head tipped to the side, his dimple appearing. "Baby, you're gonna be fine." He kissed my nose. "I'll meet you for lunch; I've got an hour to spare between classes."

"Okay. Where?"

"You know the big oval library just outside the humanities building?"

My nose crinkled.

"I took you there yesterday. You'll know what I'm talking about when you see it. Just use the map I gave you. I'll be waiting for you there."

"Okay."

"One o'clock."

"Got it."

He smiled down at me, his eyes lighting with glee. "It's so good to have you here, Ella."

"Yeah, it's good to be here." I didn't mean a word of it, but I smiled, my tongue just sticking past my front teeth. "Have a nice shower."

He gave me one more quick kiss before scurrying into the bathroom. I could picture David's lean body hopping beneath the spray. I'd explored every inch of that guy, run my fingers over his contours and kissed his lips a thousand times.

So why then, did a guy I'd never even seen make my insides burn?

I swallowed, blocking him from my mind and trying to focus back on my day.

Breakfast.

First class.

Man, I hoped I made it to both. I thought about the neatly-folded map in my purse and cringed. David didn't know me at all if he thought I was capable of reading the damn thing.

I turned left and then suddenly remembered I was supposed to have gone right. Spinning on my heel, I lifted my eyes to the sky and wished I was back in the safety of a shower stall, listening to the most luscious voice I'd ever heard.

SEVEN

COLE

Her voice felt wrong for some reason. I knew it was a stupid thing to think. Singing voices and speaking voices were very different, but the further I walked with Caroline, the more unsettled I felt. But it had to be her. We would have been the only people in the shower at that time.

I now knew the girl was a junior and majoring in business studies, like me. We chatted about that for a few minutes, but I wanted to get to the point. I had to confirm she was my shower girl before asking her out on a date.

Her steps slowed as she reached her door, and I put my free hand in my pocket, suddenly feeling awkward. "Well, I guess I just wanted to tell you that you have a beautiful voice."

"Thanks." Her brow wrinkled again, her brown eyes narrowing with confusion.

I grinned. "I bet you never sing in public, do you? Save it all up for the shower?"

"The shower? What?" Her pointy nose scrunched up and I knew.

This wasn't my shower bird.

Taking a step back, I ran a hand through my hair and looked to the ground. My chuckle was breathy and embarrassed. It took me a second to look back up at her. "Sorry, I just, um, saw you coming out of the bathroom and was wondering if you were the type to sing in the shower."

"Not really." Her blonde hair rustled over her back. "In and out as fast as I can, usually. Got too many other things to do."

"Yeah. Yeah." I swallowed. She wasn't the one. Damn it! "Well, I better let you get on with them."

"Okay." She nodded. "But listen, if you ever want to get together or have a coffee..."

"Yeah, thanks." I nodded, forcing a grin. "I'll keep that in mind. Have a good first day, Caroline."

"You too." She still looked confused as she opened her door and glided inside.

My disappointment was sharp. Damn. Damn! How could I have approached the wrong girl? What a freaking idiot.

The sudden thought that the actual girl might still have been looking for me outside the bathrooms rushed through my head and I picked up my pace, racing down the corridor and nearly taking out two short freshman guys.

"Sorry," I mumbled as I brushed past them and came to a stop outside the bathrooms. The human traffic had increased and there were already four potential girls walking around me. It could have been any one of them, and I wasn't about to chase down the two departing figures. I eyed up the other two girls. One of them gave me a sharp frown and glared at me, while the other put on a smoldering smile.

Forget it. Songbird would never look at me like that; her voice was way too pure and sweet.

I bit back a curse and put my hands on my hips, ready to give in and head back to my room.

"Hey, man."

Glancing up, I found David walking out of the bathroom, still towel-drying his hair.

"Hey." I grinned, feeling myself relax. I needed to put shower girl out of my brain and get focused for the day. I slapped David on the back and stepped in time with him.

"How was work last night?" David glanced up at me.

"Yeah, good. Same old, same old. Nina wants you to come visit. She hasn't seen you all summer and wants to know everything you've been doing."

David grinned. "I love that woman."

"Heart of gold, right?"

"For sure." We turned toward 309.

"So, you got a full day ahead?"

"Yeah, a meeting and then two classes before lunch. Oh hey," David looked back at me as he swung our door open. "Can you meet me for lunch?"

"I don't see why not." I shrugged. "I have a break between twelve and three."

"Perfect. You can come and meet Ella."

"Oh, that's right." I threw my towel over the back of my desk chair. "Your girlfriend arrived yesterday."

I gave him a sly smile and he blushed.

"Yes she did, and I really want you to meet her."

She was the last person I wanted to meet. What I really wanted to do was spend my spare three hours scouring the campus for a girl with the voice of an angel, but how the hell was I supposed to do that? And what the hell was wrong with me that I even wanted to?

In an attempt to hide my lunacy, I crossed my arms and grinned at my friend. "I can do that for you, man. Where should I meet ya?"

"I'm meeting her by the library outside the humanities building."

"Oh, well, we should go to Shiffon's then. They serve great coffee there."

"Yeah, they do. Good idea."

"Well, I'll just meet you outside the library and we can walk there together."

"Sounds cool," David threw over his shoulder as he closed his door.

I did the same, trying to get my head into the right frame of mind. Pulling on my jeans and a white cotton shirt, I pushed the sleeves up to my elbows and reached under the bed for my book bag; I hadn't used the thing in weeks. Banging out the dust, I checked there was no rotting fruit hiding in the bottom and started sorting through my stuff.

Another day. Another year. Same old. Same old.

I paused.

Except it wasn't. UChicago would never be the same for me again, because now I knew that somewhere on this campus walked a perfect songbird.

EIGHT
ELLA

I drew a circle on my notepad as I listened to the professor talk through his introduction of philosophy. I had been handed so many sheets of paper this morning, I could barely keep track of them all. Assignment deadlines, course outlines, test dates — it was all shoved in my face, and I was somehow supposed to absorb it. So far, my morning had been overwhelming. Yes, I had experienced it before, but UChicago had an intensity to it that I wasn't used to.

I kept telling myself this would all be okay and not to get stressed out by the workload, but I'd have to work my ass off to keep up with all this stuff, and unlike my boyfriend, that idea didn't exactly thrill me. David loved studying; he loved the challenge and the mental stimulation. I, on the other hand, endured study for one reason only...I swore I'd get a degree. It was what my parents wanted me to do. We'd always talked about it and even though they weren't around anymore, I felt like it was something I had to follow through on. But at the end of the day, it was just going to be a piece of paper with my name on it. I had no intention of doing post-grad courses. All I wanted to do was pass, and pass well. I'd flown through my community college courses, but I had a feeling this would be much tougher.

My circle grew bigger and I started adding starbursts around the edges. I always doodled when I got bored. It wasn't that philosophy was mind-numbingly dull; I knew I'd learn a lot of cool stuff, but this was my third lecture of the day and my brain was done.

I wondered if I was taking something else whether I'd be feeling this way. How cool would it be to do something a little more entertaining...like singing, but there's no way in Hades I'd attempt that. Jody and Morgan were the only people to have ever heard me sing...and I guess shower guy.

My cheeks heated with color. I couldn't help it!

It had been so incredibly cool singing with him this morning. I hadn't felt that kind of exhilarating joy since before my parents had passed. The all-too-familiar sadness settled on me as the professor's words turned to fuzz, and I was exported back to 2009. Although this time the memory started a little earlier in the day. As if bursting from its hiding place, it flooded my mind with color and music.

Mom laughed, throwing her head back as Dad spun her around the living room. Their dance classes were paying off, and I smiled as I stretched my voice over the long note and then clipped it off so the music could take the lead. I shuffled from one foot to the other, clicking my fingers to the beat of "Come Fly With Me." My parents were squeezing in one more practice before they left for class, and I happily volunteered to sing for them.

"You're next, sugar," Dad called over Mom's shoulder, winking at me.

I laughed, excited about my turn. Dad was teaching me all the moves and I was loving it. None of my friends knew that I could dance like a dame from the 40s, but I could and I had to admit, I was getting kind of good.

I finished the song with a flourish, lifting my arm and sticking out my chin. My parents laughed, out of breath as they clapped me down from my perch on the sofa.

Mom kissed my forehead and rubbed my back. "I knew I named you after Ella for a reason. You have the voice of an angel, and you're my own little songbird." She grinned, moving out of the way so I could step into Dad's arms.

He straightened me up, reminding me to keep my frame strong while Mom scrolled through her laptop, choosing an upbeat version of "Anything Goes." Cole Porter was a genius.

I giggled as Dad swung me around, lifting my tiny body up so I could swing around past him. Following his lead, we skimmed across the floor as if it were made of glass. I felt like I could fly, lost in a perfect moment.

An hour later, I stood at the door waving them off, promising that I would finish my homework and get to bed on time. I closed the door as they started pulling out of the driveway and did my little alone dance before prancing into the kitchen. Pulling out the gummy bears, I snitched a handful and danced up the stairs, popping them into my mouth as I hummed "Puttin' On The Ritz."

I rushed through my homework, wanting to get it done so I could watch Friday Night Lights *before bed. It was sitting on the hard drive, patiently waiting for me to catch up with the latest episode.*

It was awesome and I walked up to bed a-buzz, brushing my teeth and swooning over Taylor Kitsch. Man, he was a hottie! I dreamed of him running off the football field and kissing my lips after a game as I spun my way to the bedroom and stripped off my clothes. I glanced at my clock as I snuggled under my sheets and reached for my book. My parents would be home soon, and I wanted to stay awake to hear how their class went. They loved it so much and always came home on a high.

A banging on the door jolted me awake. The book fell out of my hands and thumped on the floor. I squinted around my room, a little disoriented, and then heard the knocking again.

The door.

Who the hell was at my door?

I reached for my watch and checked the time as I shuffled down the stairs. Why wasn't Dad answering the door already? It was nearly midnight.

I fumbled down the stairs and with a sigh, shifted the curtain covering the glass so I could peek outside. My heart stopped beating. I'm sure it did, because everything in my body went numb as I breathlessly wrapped my fingers around the door handle and pulled it open.

Two officers dressed in blue towered over me, their faces grim.

"Ella Simmons?"

I nodded.

"I'm really sorry, but you're gonna need to come with us."

"So make sure you've finished the first three readings by the time you come back here." Professor Williams's voice jolted me out of my nightmare. I swallowed, looking at the person next to me and quickly deciphering their scribble. I jotted down what we had to get through and flipped my binder closed. My heart was hammering the way it always did after my memories took me.

Sliding the textbook over my little table, I hugged it to my chest and closed my eyes. Thank God I was about to meet David for lunch; he always knew how to calm my rattled nerves. When I'd first moved from Washington, meeting Jody and Morgan had been a life-saver, but David had given me something the girls couldn't...a sense of security. He was so focused and knew exactly where he was going. I loved that about him. I loved that I could take his hand and follow in his wake, not having to think about my future. The fact I didn't know what I really wanted scared me, and it was easier just to go along with David's plans.

Unlike most people, new things terrified me and David never made me feel bad for that. He was always happy to take the lead and look after me. Even when he left for college and I thought I wouldn't be able to cope, I was okay. He Skyped or emailed me daily. He called me every day, just like he said he would, and every holiday, he flew home to be with me. David equaled safety, and even though moving to Chicago was unsettling—and if I was one-hundred-percent honest, I didn't really want to be here—I knew it was the best place for me. I belonged by David's side, and no shower man or workload was going to stop me from believing that.

Following the trail of students out the double doors, I skipped down the steps and wondered which way to turn. I knew I should have asked for directions. Everyone walking past me probably knew exactly where the big oval library was, but I was too shy...or proud. No, shy. I was definitely too embarrassed to have to ask, and so I pressed my lips together and wandered off to the right. I circled the entire humanities building, my stress increasing with each step. I finally found the backside of the library and rolled my eyes. If I'd just turned left, I would have been there in about a minute flat.

Gripping my bag strap, I walked around the edge, glancing at my watch and hoping David would forgive my lateness. I knew he hated being late, and he only had an hour to spare. I chewed on my bottom lip as I made my way around the edge and finally spotted him.

He was standing next to a tall guy with dark brown curls. Holy cow, he was beautiful. He looked like Superman. In all seriousness. His fitted, white shirt accentuated his broad chest and muscular arms. He stood casually with his hands in his pockets, his chiseled face reminding me of a Roman aristocrat. His blue eyes scanned his surroundings as he waited for David to finish up his phone call. He spotted me walking toward him, the edge of his mouth tipping at the side. He didn't have any dimples, but his smile was to die for.

I broke eye contact, scared I might actually drown in his blue gaze. Clearing my throat, I glanced back up in time to see him nudging David in the side. My boyfriend spun and caught sight of me approaching. Quickly ending his call, he walked toward me and flung his arm over my shoulder.

"Hey, baby. How was your morning?" He kissed my forehead.

"Good. I didn't get lost, which was good."

He chuckled. "Not until you were trying to find me, right?"

We came to a stop beside Superman and I winced. "Sorry for being late."

"That's okay." David squeezed my shoulder. "I knew you'd get a little lost."

I tried not to let the comment bother me, but it

kind of did. Especially since he said it right in front of his friend. I drew in a breath and gave them both a closed-mouth smile.

"Anyway, this is my roommate, Cole."

I reached for his outstretched hand and shook it. His large fingers were warm and wrapped around mine in a gentle, yet confident shake. "Nice to meet you, Ella." His voice was deep and smooth, and I couldn't help smiling.

"You too."

He let go of my hand and I quickly reached for David's, needing to erase the tingles buzzing over my skin. What the hell was wrong with me? First shower guy, now Cole! Why was I attracted to all these other men, when the only one I really wanted was walking right beside me?

I let their carefree chatter wash over me as we walked to the cafe, trying to keep my eyes straight ahead and not let my gaze wander to the powerful shoulders moving in my peripheral vision. I squeezed David's hand as we walked, a constant reminder that there was only one man for me.

NINE

COLE

I couldn't take my eyes off Ella. It was bad. I felt like some star-struck kid who was staring at a world-famous celebrity.

There was just something so beautiful about the way she moved and the softness of her voice. Her hazel eyes watched me carefully as I spoke, and the questions she asked made it obvious she heard everything I said.

Pure sunshine, that was the only way to describe her smile. She'd obviously had braces as a kid, because her teeth were perfectly straight. Her angular nose had a cute point at the end. It wasn't too long, just right for her face, and she had these gorgeous locks of mouse-brown hair that I wanted to run my fingers through.

I didn't realize what a lucky guy David was. That photo on his bulletin board didn't do her justice, probably because there was an essence about her that could only be captured in the flesh. I averted my gaze as she looked up from her milkshake. She hadn't ordered anything to eat. She was a petite, skinny thing and looked as though she didn't eat much. Her narrow finger brushed away her milk moustache. As she spotted someone past my shoulder, her face lit with another smile that I couldn't turn away from.

"Hey." She raised her hand with a wave and stood. I glanced behind me and noticed Morgan and her boyfriend, Brad, sauntering toward us. The guy was like a tank. I'd heard he was into the gym big time and it really showed.

I didn't see these two very often. Morgan and David weren't the best of friends, but it looked like Ella was a different story. She squeezed Morgan tight and held her at arm's length.

"How was your morning?"

"Totally fine." Morgan brushed her off. "I'm more interested in yours."

"It was great."

There was a strain in Ella's voice, and I could tell that Morgan didn't believe her. Her eyes narrowed slightly, and Ella gave her a stiff head shake. I glanced at David to see if he was noticing this, but he was caught up shaking hands with Brad.

"Sit down. Join us."

"Cool. Thanks." Brad pulled out a chair and slumped down, giving Ella a little smile.

Morgan perched on her seat and waved to the waitress. The woman came over and Ella's tall friend ordered two coffees.

"You want anything to eat, babe?" Morgan turned to her boyfriend.

"Yeah, actually, bring me a BLT, please," he said

to the waitress.

She wrote it down and looked to Morgan. "You want anything?"

Morgan looked at Ella's milkshake and then shook her head. "No, I'm good."

Ella touched her arm. "You should have something if you want."

"No, it's fine, I can eat later."

I thought it was weird. Were these two on some kind of diet or something? I wanted to ask, pry, find out everything I could about the petite brunette across from me, but it wasn't my business, so I sealed my lips and looked to the table.

Ella hadn't let David's hand go since we were introduced. She kept rubbing her thumb over his knuckles and squeezing his hand like a lifeline. It was like she was afraid to let go, and I wondered why. She seemed a timid, tentative person. There was a fragility about her that wasn't unappealing. She didn't look like the high-maintenance, possessive kind, just unsure of herself. I could understand why David was so protective of her.

If I had a girl that sweet and pretty, I'd want to protect her too.

The photograph of her tucked under David's arm came to mind again. If she was my girl, that picture would not be hidden under piles of study papers; I'd have it displayed front and center so I could look at it every time I walked into the room.

I cleared my throat, rubbing the back of my neck and reminding myself that Ella was not my girl and never would be. I wasn't the type to muscle in on a friend's girl.

David was as loyal as they came. I would never forget the first day I got back to my room to find a new roommate setting up his stuff. I hadn't been looking forward to another shared-room experience, and I nearly moved back in with Nina and Malachi, but Nina convinced me to stay and give it one more shot.

"Dorm life can be so much fun, and you'll miss out if you live here with us."

So, I was preparing myself for another year of loud music and sloppy living. But that wasn't the case.

"Oh hey, you must be Cole." David brushed his hands on his jeans and reached out for a handshake.

He was a freshman, it was easy to see that, but he was onto it. His bright eyes and confident smile gave me hope as I shook his hand.

"So, what are the rules in this place? Do you have a space that's your own, or can I just kind of put my stuff where I like?"

I was taken back by the question; my last roommate was a selfish jerk.

"That room's mine." I pointed to the left. "As long as your stuff isn't too weird then plaster it up wherever."

"Cool. Cool. Okay, well I'm a simple guy, so I won't be putting up much." He put his hands on his hips, hesitating, and then glanced me over and shook his head. "You know, actually before I unpack, I gotta ask... You're not one of those party animal guys, are ya? 'Cause I'm really here to study and do well, so if we're gonna have a conflict of interest, maybe I should look at changing rooms."

I snickered. "Nah, man. We're cool. Let me know if you need a hand with anything." I walked toward my room, feeling a huge weight lift off my shoulders. David and I were gonna get on just fine.

He'd become a really good friend over the two years we lived together. I was glad he was sticking around for my final year, and I really hoped my replacement would be a good match for him. David was a focused guy, and I made sure I never got in the way of his study time. He was pretty particular about it and I respected that.

Man, how was he gonna cope having Ella here now? If she was mine, I wouldn't be able to concentrate on one word of any textbook. If I had my way, we'd be holed up in my room for as many minutes as we could spare.

I cut the image of her lying beneath me short, hating myself for going there. She was David's, not mine! I forced a smile when she glanced my way, and I knew it was time to split.

"Well, it was really nice to see everyone again." I stood from the table. "Ella, nice to meet you." I held out my hand. I couldn't help it, just one last touch before I washed her from my mind.

"Same here." She let go of David's hand to give mine a little squeeze, but it was only brief, and her hand was tucked straight back within David's before I'd even had a chance to push my chair in.

I dropped a few bills on the table next to David's plate and slapped him on the shoulder.

"I'll catch you later, man."

"See you 'round."

I didn't look back as I walked away. I couldn't.

Damn, why did she have to be so sweet?

This day was screwing with my head big time. What was wrong with me? My stupid chat with Nina was making me think this shit. I didn't want a relationship.

"Oh really? Then why did you just spend your entire lunch time pining for what your best friend's got?" I mumbled under my breath, shoving my hands into my pockets. What would it be like to have one hand free, clasping the fingers of some sweet girl as I walked her to her next class?

It would be damn nice.

"No it wouldn't!"

The girl beside me jolted to a stop and gave me a

strange look.

"Sorry," I muttered, forcing a smile and walking past her.

I let out a heavy sigh and took the steps two at a time, planning on cutting through the humanities building. My next class wasn't until three, which gave me an hour to walk around campus and not think of Ella.

As each minute ticked past it became more and more clear. I wanted a girl, but not just any girl, and since I couldn't have Ella, there was only one possible solution left.

I had to find my songbird.

TEN

ELLA

I pushed the door open with my shoulder and closed it with my butt. Dumping my binder and water bottle down on the spare desk next to our mini-fridge, I dropped my bag to the floor and slumped on the couch with a sigh.

Pressing my head back into the cushions, I closed my eyes and tried not to let David's text bug me.

He was bailing. Again.

Friday night was mine. That was what he'd said to me in my first week here. Well, I'd been here five weeks now, and I'd only had two Fridays with him. I never realized just how obsessed my boyfriend was with studying; it pissed me off. He made me come all the way over here, leave a little college I loved, come to this big-ass school with its high-ass pressure, and then he wasn't even around to spend time with me!

I knew he didn't make me come, but it felt like it some days.

Running my thumb over the screen, I read the text again and dropped the phone next to me. I didn't want to reply; I couldn't be bothered. I knew what I'd say...something really sweet and understanding about how it was so much more important for him to study for Monday's test than spend time with his girlfriend.

The phone beeped again.

I can tell you're annoyed. I really am sorry, but this is a big one. I might be able to squeeze you in for dinner tomorrow night. I'll make it up to you. Promise.

"Squeeze me in," I muttered. "Thanks." I wanted to drop the phone again and ignore his text, but me being me, rolled my eyes and then tapped the screen, replying...

I understand.
Not!
Just text me when you're ready for a break tomorrow and I'll pop over.

"Because I'm your personal slave, and I don't know how to tell you how mad I really am."

I sent the text and bit the edge of my lip.

"What's up with you?"

Morgan stepped from her room looking gorgeous. Being with Brad was really doing wonders for her. Morgan was a big lady and had struggled with her weight in the past, but dating a gym junkie was motivating her to eat well and exercise. Her tall, curvaceous frame was stunning in her little black dress with high heels. She never usually wore heels that high. I raised my eyebrows.

"I know." She cringed. "I'll probably regret it the second I walk out the door, but I felt like being brave."

I grinned. "You look amazing."

"I'm gonna be taller than Brad in these things."

"Barely! You guys will look super-hot standing next to each other. Where are you going?"

"He's taking me to Bird's Nest for dinner then we're heading to Quigg's for a little dancing." She wiggled her hips, making me laugh. "There's a band playing there tonight. Chaos. I heard them just before the summer break and they're amazing. They're only in high school, too. It's pretty impressive." She clipped her purse closed and slipped it onto her shoulder. "What are you doing tonight?"

"I don't know." I pouted. "I might get into my jim-jams and watch a movie."

"What?" Morgan threw her arms wide. "It's Friday night. You can't just sit at home. Where's David?"

"Studying."

"Again?" Her eyebrows shot north. This was extra ammo for her, and I so didn't need that.

"Come on, Morgan. He's got a really big test on Monday, and you know he wants to pass with an A+ average this year."

"That is so ridiculous. He needs a life. I thought when you got here he might get better, but he's still obsessed with his plan."

"It's a good plan." I shrugged.

"Ella, good plans involve a little flexibility." Morgan's hands were now on her hips. Not a good sign.

I looked away, scratching my right eyebrow and trying to bring the conversation to an end.

Morgan sat down next to me with a little sigh. "You know this band, Chaos, they do a mix of covers and their own stuff. They're really good if you want to come check them out." She squeezed my knee. "You should meet us there at nine. We'll shake our asses on the dance floor."

"I don't know." My nose wrinkled.

"Oh come on, Ella Bella! Come have fun with me." She made a face, the cute, adorable one that made her look like a little kid again.

I grinned. "Maybe."

"You better." She pointed at me, standing from the couch and adjusting her dress. "I'll be looking out for you the second I walk through that pub door, you hear me?"

"I hear ya," I called over my shoulder as she walked out the door. "Have fun!"

Slumping back onto the couch, I gazed at the TV remote perched on the coffee table and pursed my lips. Staying here was easier; I hated going out on my own.

"I miss Cali." I pouted again, like a stupid little five-year-old. I was so pathetic sometimes.

But I did miss Cali. If I was in Pasadena right now, Jody and I would be doing something fun together. She never let me just sit on my butt and feel sorry for myself.

Glancing at my watch, I quickly calculated the time difference and reached for my laptop. I dialed up Jody on Skype and tapped my finger, hoping her online status actually meant she was around.

"Ells Bells! What are you doing calling me?" Her bubbly voice reached me before her image did. I watched the dial spin and then up popped my blonde friend, her green eyes bright and cheerful.

"Hey, Jo-Jo." I waved.

"Whatchya doin'?" Her straight white teeth appeared.

"Just hanging in my room."

"What?" Her smile disappeared. "Ella, it's Friday night. Unless David is currently in your bed naked, you should be out right now."

I giggled, feeling my cheeks heat with color. "David has to study tonight, so I'm flying solo."

"Well, call a friend, go out!"

"Morgan's on a date. I don't want to play third wheel."

"What about your other friends?"

"What other friends?"

"Are you kidding me right now?" Her mouth dropped open. "Ella Simmons, you have been there for over a month. What have you been doing with your time?"

"Studying."

"That's it?" Jody groaned.

"David's taken me out a couple of times." I sat up straighter, trying to stand up for my loser lifestyle.

"Honey, come on. You are hiding and you know it. When was the last time you wore makeup?"

"What has that got to do with anything?"

"Makeup equals going out, and going out means spending time with other people and having fun."

"I...you know I'm not great at making friends. I'm too shy."

"Stop hiding behind that excuse!"

"I always used to rely on you and Morgan. I'm not good at this stuff."

"Well, get it together then. Practice makes perfect. Believe me, I know." Her exasperated voice made me smile.

"How are rehearsals going?"

"They're great. They're fun, but I'm so tired. Between dance class, singing lessons, learning lines and rehearsals coming out my backside, I don't have a life at the moment," she whined.

"At least you're hanging out with people you like."

"That is true and if the cast weren't so damn cool, I'd be pulling my hair out in clumps."

"The trials of being talented." I tipped my head and winked.

Jody laughed at me before gazing at her watch. Her eyes bulged. "Babe, I'm sorry. I gotta go in a sec."

"Okay." I tried to hide my disappointment behind a broad grin, but I wasn't fooling anyone.

Leaning toward the camera, Jody's stern face filled the screen. "You have to promise me that you will go out tonight."

I cringed.

"Ella, you have to promise or I'm not leaving, and then I'll be late and I'll get in trouble and it'll be your fault."

I poked out my tongue at her. She pressed her lips together, squashing her grin.

Relenting with a sigh, I finally said, "Morgan asked me to join her and Brad at this pub to go dancing."

"Perfect! You love dancing."

"Not in front of people."

"But you're so good. Screw your courage to the sticking place, girl."

"Throwing Shakespeare at me is not going to get me off this couch."

"Your butt twitched when I said that. I can tell." She pointed at her camera.

Giggles shook my tummy, but I held them at bay.

"Forget your inhibitions, Ella. Stop watching people live out these awesome lives on screen and go and do it yourself!"

"What if I get lost?"

"You won't. What's this place called?"

"Quigg's."

"Google it. Use Google maps."

"I can't read maps."

"You don't have to. Google maps will show you which bus or train to take...or just get the address and grab a cab."

I knew she was right. I wasn't that stupid, but I wanted to be. It would have been the perfect excuse to get out of this.

"What if Morgan and Brad don't show?"

"Then introduce yourself to someone new, dumbass."

I snickered and scratched my forehead, running out of options. It looked like I was going out tonight.

"Now stop stalling and go suit up! Wear something that makes you feel sexy. I don't care that David's not there. You turn heads tonight, girl."

"Love you, Jo-Jo. Wish you were here."

"So do I." Her tender smile made my eyes well with tears. "Go make me proud. I expect a selfie on my phone within the next two hours. I want proof that you did it."

"Okay." I winced, making Jody chuckle as she hung up on the call.

I closed the laptop and felt the silence descend around me. Looking across the empty room, I let out a slow sigh before rising from the couch and walking to my room. Pulling open my closest, I scanned my row of neatly hung jeans and shook my head.

"Turn heads, not be invisible." My lips twitched. "But I like being invisible."

I put my hand on my hip and dropped my shoulders.

"Get a life, Ella."

Hangers banged against one another as I flicked through my wardrobe and finally came to a stop by my one pair of black leather pants. Morgan called them my *Grease* gear and started singing "You're The One That I Want" whenever I put them on.

"I got chills, they're multiplying," I sung with a chuckle.

Pulling them out, I quickly undressed and wiggled into them before I could change my mind.

Forty-five minutes later, my lashes were lacquered, my lips were glossed and my torso was wrapped in a purple V-neck shirt. My necklaces clinked against each other as I clipped my way to the door. I double-checked that Quigg's address was on my phone screen before drawing in a deep breath and braving the unknown.

ELEVEN

COLE

"Hand me that mic stand."

I passed it over to Jimmy before lifting the amp and placing it next to Ralphie's bass guitar.

"Thanks, man." The sixteen-year-old crouched down and plugged in his beloved instrument.

"We nearly ready for a sound check, guys?" Jimmy, the lead singer, turned to the rest of the band and waited for confirmation from each of them.

Nessa, the cutest drummer this world has ever seen, adjusted her seat and banged the bass pedal a couple of times. "Nearly." Her little button nose twitched as she shifted her kit into exactly the right position. She finally looked up with a nod.

Jimmy adjusted the microphone, strumming his

guitar once. Satisfied, he turned back to Ness with a short nod.

"Okay, here we go." She banged her sticks together and launched into "Ocean Avenue" by Yellowcard.

They sounded good, and I couldn't help grinning as I stood next to their loyal tech man, Quinn. He came to every gig, helping them out on the sidelines. I slapped him on the shoulder and nodded my approval.

Chaos seemed to be getting better and better. I first heard them play last year when Jimmy's older brother invited me along to the school talent quest. I didn't usually go to that kind of stuff, but Troy and I had been close in high school, and he was trying to rally as much support for his kid brother as possible. I was so glad I went. Hearing those kids rock the stage was inspiring. The next day, I asked Malachi if they could play at Quigg's sometime. Their age made him reluctant, but he eventually conceded, and he let them play a couple of lunch gigs. It pulled a pretty big crowd and this year, Malachi agreed to make them monthly regulars.

The pub was already filling up. People had come early for dinner and were enjoying the sound check, getting excited about the entertainment to come.

"Make sure some of those tables are pulled back so there's a little dancing room," Nina shouted into my ear as she walked past. I nodded and did as commanded, getting Frankie's help to shift the two empty tables back a notch. The dance space was pretty small, but it'd be enough for people to move around.

Flick, the other guitarist, cut the check short. "Just give me a sec to re-tune."

He began to fiddle while the rest of the band

made their own last-minute adjustments. Jimmy walked over to Ralphie, chatting about the playlist, and I tuned out. I needed to get back to the bar in a second; it would be a busy night and I wanted to be on my game.

"Hey, Cole."

I spun around at the soft voice, not sure whom it belonged to. I stared at her. There was something familiar about the way she was looking at me, but it took me a minute to place her. The napkin. The phone number. That was it.

I forced a bright smile. "Oh, hey, Candace. How's it going?"

"Good. Just thought I'd pop by and see ya again."

I pushed out a laugh. "Yeah, well, I'm not sure I'll have that much time to socialize; it's gonna be a busy one tonight."

Heading back to the bar, I ducked beneath it and popped up on the other side, glad to have the wood between me and the blonde bombshell.

"You never called." Her upper teeth brushed her lower lip and I felt a little bad.

"Yeah, I'm sorry about that." Clearing my throat, I reached for a towel and flung it over my shoulder. "I'm pretty swamped with school at the moment."

She shrugged. "I get it." Her gaze was sad, which only made me feel worse.

Although the school thing was actually true. This final year was turning out to be a real bitch. I hated studying and was forcing myself through each lecture. A huge part of me wanted to quit and just get on with setting up my own pub. My inheritance was healthy. I had full access to it now, but Nina made me promise to graduate first and I knew I couldn't let her down.

I pursed my lips, feeling awkward that Candace

was still standing there gazing at me.

"Well, I better get on with it."

"Yeah, see you 'round, Cole." She turned away with a little pout, and I looked to the ceiling. I hated hurting her feelings, but I seriously was not interested in what she had to offer.

My mind had done a complete 180 since that day in the shower. Casual flings were no longer good enough. I wanted an actual relationship now, and it bugged the heck out of me. I had been trying to talk myself out of it, reminding myself that only full-blown lunatics thought this way, but I just couldn't seem to shake the need. I felt ready to move on with my life and take that next step into adulthood. It was frickin' absurd.

I blamed it on my songbird. Her voice had stuck with me, following me into my dreams. I shoved the image out of my mind and Ella appeared instead. Ella, the sweet, quiet girl who'd somehow filtered into my thoughts more than I'd wanted her to over the last month. I didn't want to think about her. I *shouldn't* have been thinking about her. She was in a relationship. Not just any relationship, but a committed one with my roommate. If any girl on campus should have been considered off-limits, it was Ella.

I had bumped into her a few times, but we'd never really had time to stop and chat...which was a good thing. As much as I liked the idea of a friendship with her, I knew it'd be more than challenging.

If only I could find shower girl.

It wasn't from a lack of trying. I'd returned to the shower the same time every morning for over a week, hoping to catch her. After that, I switched it up, squeezing in a shower whenever I could on the off-chance she might have been there, which she never was. There was of course the possibility that she just wasn't singing back, but I didn't like to entertain that thought. Surely she'd been affected as much as I had. I wasn't trying to be arrogant, just hopeful, I guess.

My spirits had slowly deflated with each passing day. I'd been keeping my eyes peeled whenever I walked the third floor of my dorm, but the only thing to really catch my eyes was Ella.

I tried to convince myself that there were plenty of other college girls just as pretty as Ella, and who knew what my shower songbird really even looked like. She could be missing a freaking limb or her two front teeth. She could be bald. Worse than that, she could be a total bitch. I was a fool to think that two songs could tell me everything I needed to know, but damn, it'd be cool to find out. Something about her sweet sound kept me veering back to this new course I'd insensibly set for myself.

My depressing reverie was cut short by Jimmy.

"Hey, everybody. We're Chaos. Thanks so much for coming out to hear us tonight. We hope you'll have a little fun!" He raised his arm and Nessa kicked in with a thumping beat that grew to a kick-ass version of "So What" by Pink.

A grin stretched across my face. Troy would be so proud right now. Jimmy had been a bit of a train wreck before Troy bought him a guitar. The wild child had been tamed...sort of. Grabbing my phone, I raised it above the cheering crowd and snapped a picture, texting it to Troy in L.A.

Slipping it back into my pocket, I turned to the sound of a drink order and got to work.

I was soon pulling beers and pouring tequila shots, checking IDs and having a blast behind the bar. It was so much easier to shove my troubles aside with this much noise in the room. Placing a beer down, I grabbed the money off the counter and thanked the guy, looking over his shoulder as the door pushed open.

My easy smile faltered as Miss Off Limits slipped into the room, looking so damn hot my lips actually parted.

Holy shit.

Was that even the same girl?

Her big, hazel eyes scanned the room, her lips pressing together as she gently shut the door behind her. Her straight teeth caught the edge of her glossy lip and I grinned. Oh yeah, there she was.

I couldn't help it. A slow smile stretched across my face as the sexy little thing took a tentative step toward the bar.

TWELVE

ELLA

I did it.

I made it, all by myself. I was so incredibly proud, which only made me feel ridiculous. So I'd managed to catch a cab and give the driver an address. How lame was that.

The music was thumping from the pub, an instant beat running through me. I loved the sound immediately, my spirit lifting as I opened the door. It didn't seem to matter what kind of music was playing; melody did things to me, made me feel alive.

Closing the door gently behind me, I scanned the room, hoping to see Morgan's blonde hair above the crowd, but I couldn't spot her. I bit my lip like I always did and took a cautious step toward the bar. In spite of my heels, I still went up on my tiptoes to see if I could find her, but she wasn't there.

Crap! What the hell did I do now?

Nerves got the better of me as I inched my way into the room. I couldn't leave before taking a selfie or Jody would never let me hear the end of it. Maybe if I just perched my butt on a bar stool, took a quick shot and then left. I could get away with that.

Squeezing past a couple of tall guys with beers in their hands, I mumbled, "Excuse me" and worked my way to the bar. There was one spare stool, right near the end. My head spun with relief as I made my way toward it. Climbing up, I let my feet dangle as I scrambled for my phone.

I was such a chicken.

I ran my thumb over my phone screen and wondered if I should text Morgan first. If she was only a couple of minutes away then maybe I could hold out. My foot tapped of its own accord as I unlocked my phone. The band had a really awesome sound and I wanted to stay and hear a little more. My thumb hovered over the green Messages button. I glanced to the door, hoping Morgan might appear before I sent her an SOS.

"Can I get you something?"

I jerked at the male voice behind me and spun around. "No, thanks, I'm not old enough to dri—" I smiled, a big broad one that strained my lips. It was probably bred more from relief than anything. Cole. A face I knew! I wanted to kiss him. Not because I was attracted to him of course, just because I was relieved. I inwardly cringed at my lie, hoping it wouldn't show through in my smile. "I didn't know you worked here," I shouted above the music.

"I know the owners." His gorgeous eyes danced

as he gazed at me.

"Nice." I couldn't rip my eyes away from him. He was so incredibly gorgeous. His chiseled jaw. Those high cheekbones...and the little dimple on his chin, which, now that I could see it properly, actually appeared to be a scar. It was sexy. I didn't know why something that was probably created by an open wound and stitches could be so attractive, but it was. I wanted to run my finger over it and find out the story. I wanted to hear his sheepish chuckle and watch his skin heat as he launched into the details.

Curling my fingers together, I pressed them into my lap. I didn't have the right to touch him. That luxury would one day belong to another girl.

I still couldn't believe he didn't have a girlfriend. I nearly fell off my chair when David had told me.

"You know, we do serve sodas here." He winked.

My nerves began to settle as I took in his friendly expression. It was so obvious he was a good guy, and if I had to spend my night chatting to him, I wouldn't have minded a bit.

"Right. Of course you do. Can I please have a Sprite with lots of ice?"

"Coming right up." I watched him work behind the bar, his movements fluid and confident. He took other orders as he was digging out ice cubes for me, calling out something to the older man at the end of the bar. The man called out something in a thick, Irish accent, raising his hand to acknowledge Cole's comment.

I strained to hear what was said next, but it was impossible as the band started up another loud number. I couldn't help swaying to the beat just a little.

Slapping down a cardboard coaster, Cole placed the drink in front of me. "It's on the house."

"Are you sure?"

"Of course! Welcome to Quigg's." He grinned.

"Thank you."

His dancing blue eyes held me captive as he leaned over and pressed his forearms against the bar. I watched his thick muscles ripple and averted my gaze, pulling a quick sip through my straw.

He leaned toward me with a conspiratorial smile. "You know, I would have served you a drink, if you'd asked."

"Well, that is very irresponsible of you." My teasing tone took me by surprise and I cleared my throat, feeling self-conscious.

He chuckled. "You really are a good girl, aren't you?"

"Is that bad?" My nose wrinkled. I hated the way it did that.

He paused, his blue gaze softening. "No, it's actually..." he looked down with a grin and swallowed before glancing up at me again. "Refreshing."

I smiled and raised my glass, taking another sip. The man behind Cole's shoulder called his attention, and he was dragged away from me. I stayed where I was, sipping my soda and watching Cole work. His friendly smile was endearing, and I loved the way he looked people in the eye as he spoke to them. I saw a few flirty gestures thrown his way, but he didn't seem fazed by any of them. He kept glancing over at me, giving me a reassuring smile that made my insides dance. For once it wasn't a nervous dance, but an excited, giddy one that made me forget all about my boyfriend.

As the minutes ticked by I stopped looking at my watch and started to think that if Morgan and Brad never showed up, I would have been okay.

THIRTEEN
COLE

Sexy.

I'd wanted to say that her being a good girl was sexy.

Because to me, it was. Her sweet smile, her innocent look. She was a total turn on. I couldn't wrap my head around it. Unlike so many girls I encountered, she'd never throw herself at me. Her purity was attractive, which felt weird, but true.

Malachi eyed me from the other end of the bar, his eyebrows bobbing as he checked out my favorite customer. I gave him a quick glare that told him to stop being so obvious. He chuckled, slapping my back and making sure he kept his tail down the opposite end of the bar.

I finally had a second to breathe, so I headed

back to Ella.

"Can I get you a refill?"

She popped down her empty glass and held in a chuckle. Her cheeks turned bright red as she crunched through a piece of ice.

I laughed. "An ice eater. Interesting."

She swallowed her mouthful with a laugh. "David hates it, but it just tastes so good and it's all Sprite-like and sweet now."

"It doesn't bother me. Crunch away." I leaned my hands against the bar, watching her with a grin.

She smiled back. It wasn't as shy and tentative as before, and I was glad she felt more relaxed.

"So, are you meeting David here?" I had to ask. If my best friend was about to walk through the door, I wanted a heads-up.

"No." She frowned. "He has to study for some big test on Monday."

"Flying solo then, huh?"

"Kind of." She leaned closer to me so she didn't have to yell so loud. "I'm supposed to be meeting Morgan and Brad. They were telling me about Chaos." She pointed over at the small stage area. "They're really awesome!"

"Yeah, they are. I found them at a talent quest last year."

"You found them?"

I blushed, wishing I hadn't worded it that way.

"Are you their manager or something?"

"Not quite! I just like to convince Malachi to let bands play here. Liven the place up a bit."

"Well, it's working. I bet your boss loves you for it."

I looked over my shoulder at the tall Irishman and grinned. "I hope so."

Ella's sunshine smile took over her face, and I swear I wanted to freeze time.

"Oh my gosh, Ella!" Morgan's voice made us

both turn. We looked over to see her brush past the table and rush up to Ella's side. "I'm so sorry we're late. We couldn't catch a cab!"

Brad trundled in behind Morgan, raising his eyebrows at me and lifting his finger.

"What's your flavor?" I called to him.

"I'll start with a bottle of Bud."

"You got it." I turned to fill the order, watching Ella out of the corner of my eye. Her hand was on Morgan's arm, her head shaking as Morgan apologized again.

"It's really fine. Cole's been keeping me company." She flicked her thumb at me. Morgan looked over Ella's head and gave me a grateful smile. If only she knew how much I'd been enjoying it.

"Come on, Ella Bella! Let's dance."

I grinned at the nickname. Morgan took her little friend's hand and they trotted off to the dance floor. Brad took the vacant seat and lifted his bottle. "What's the bet I don't even get through half of this before she drags my ass out there."

I laughed with him, but couldn't understand what he was complaining about.

I would have done anything to be out on that dance floor. I moved so I could see Ella through the crowd. Morgan was into it, jiggling away with fluid moves that surprised me. She was really good. Ella watched her with a grin, slowly warming up and copying her talented friend. My eyebrows rose as I watched her leather-clad legs move around the floor. She was pretty damn good, too.

It was easy to sense their closeness as they laughed away together. Morgan lifted her hands, letting out a whoop. Chaos continued to rock out, the girls building up a quick sweat. I felt my body ignite as I watched Ella dip to the floor then bounce back up again. I imagined what it would feel like to have her slide beneath my hands or press against my body as I stood behind her, swaying to the beat.

The glass in my hand grew slippery, and I nearly spilled the beer all over myself before quickly slamming it onto the bar. I yelled my apologies to the customer and took their money, ringing it up with shaking hands.

"You all right, Boy-o?"

"Yep, all good." I cleared my throat and forced a grin at Malachi.

His eyes narrowed, and I had no choice but to ignore him. This wasn't cool. I was fantasizing about David's girlfriend. I needed to get my head straight.

"Just taking a quick break!" I pointed at the bathroom and Malachi gave a short nod.

I knew I'd have to be fast.

Shouldering the door open, I walked to the urinal and did my business. It felt good to have tiles in front of me and not a sexy body that made my loins ache. I washed my hands and splashed some water on my face, gazing at my warped reflection in the aging mirror before me.

"You are so screwed." I pressed my hands against the edge of the sink and sighed.

I had to find shower girl. I had to find her fast or I was going to go mentally insane.

FOURTEEN

ELLA

I arrived home on a high. Handing the taxi driver too much, I told him to keep the change and chuckled as I jumped out the door and headed into my dorm.

It was mostly quiet with only a few stragglers making their way home at this late hour. I checked my watch — 1:34 a.m. Man, what a night! I could have danced until the sun came up. It had taken me a while to warm up and not be so self-conscious. I just did that thing Jody told me to do and pretended like Morgan and I were the only people in the room. After that, I got into it and had so much fun. Chaos was kicking it, big time. Thanks to Morgan's extra-loud cheering, we got in a few requests and danced our way through some old favorites, remembering the moves we'd choreographed as teens. It was hilarious and my stomach was sore from all the laughing.

Quigg's had closed at midnight, and I'd been too pumped to think about going home, so I'd stuck around to help clean up until Nina kicked me out, insisting I catch a taxi before it got too late. Man, she was a cool chick. Cole was lucky to work for such nice people.

"Cole," I murmured his name with a dreamy smile. Unlocking the door, I stumbled into my empty room. Morgan and Brad had disappeared a little while before me, eyeing each other hungrily. I knew exactly what they were up to right now. I chuckled, flopping onto the couch with a sigh.

I wasn't physically drunk, but I felt euphoric. I was high on life and Jody would be so proud. I wanted to call her, but knew she'd be in bed already. Rehearsals were zapping all her energy and she needed her sleep. Pulling out my phone, I checked the couple of selfies I took and chose to send her the one of Morgan and me with the band. They'd been really good about posing for us at the end of the night.

"Cool kids. I wish I'd known people like that in high school."

I rolled my eyes. As if! Even if I had, I would have been too chicken to perform on stage.

I wished I had more confidence. Why was I always so scared to put myself out there?

Part of me blamed my parents' deaths. Having them ripped from my life so suddenly really did a number on me. Rather than making me strong, it made me timid, and I hadn't been able to snap out of it. Living with an overly-critical aunt hadn't helped, either. I'd been so heartbroken and terrified that I'd lost myself in the trauma. I still couldn't figure out who I was, and it was so much easier to just hide behind David and my girls. They were home to me. They were safe.

"David," I sighed, sleepily. "You missed a good night." My eyes fluttered closed as images of David swam through my head, quickly pushed aside by sexy blue eyes and dark brown curls. My fingers wove through his hair, my body stretching tall so I could reach his lips. His smile was pure magic as he pulled me close and brushed his lips against mine.

I snapped awake, jerking up from the couch. Rubbing my eyes, I held my cheeks and pulled in a breath. Not cool. Dreaming about kissing David's best friend was very not cool.

Glancing at my watch, I decided sleep was something I wouldn't capture again this morning; it was nearly five. I knew the showers would be quiet, so I raced for my stuff. I might as well get on with my day. I didn't know what it held, but I felt upbeat and figured maybe I could do some more exploring on my own. A nervous tickle of excitement ran through me.

I was humming before I even reached the shower stall. I took my standard one at the end and flicked on the spray, my voice cresting over the tune for "Steppin' Out With My Baby." I danced into the cubicle, swaying my hips and soaping myself down. I finished the song with a laugh and shifted straight into "Puttin' on the Ritz." For once, it didn't make me feel sad. It actually made me remember my parents with a smile, which then led me straight into a song that I thought of as theirs: "Someone To Watch Over Me." My thoughts swam around them as the words oozed from my body.

They would have been proud of what I did the night before. I knew they would have. It felt so good. I was proud of me. I actually grew a backbone, went out and had some fun. All by myself.

"Legend," I sung and then laughed. I was so not legendary. What I did last night, most people would do without batting an eyelid. David could do anything. He took on the world daily and never hesitated.

I picked up the rest of the song, wondering what he'd say when he found out what I'd been up to. He'd probably think it was irresponsible to have been out so late. Should I even bother telling him what I got up to? Would he feel bad because he had been stuck at home studying while I went off and lived it up with my friends?

Rinsing the shampoo out of my hair, I stood under the spray and thought for a minute.

No. He probably wouldn't be disappointed at all. He wasn't into dancing or music. He might blast his techno beats in the car and tap his finger on the steering wheel, but that was about it. He'd rather die than have to shake his tail-feathers on a dance floor. He hated that kind of stuff. He'd go to the movies with me, but nothing like what Morgan and I had been doing last night.

I wished I could share that part of myself with him, but I knew he'd think it was dumb. I didn't think I could handle any level of teasing about it. This was precious to me and needed to be protected. Man, I hoped Cole didn't say anything to him. He would. I could tell by the way he smiled at me. He'd loved how much fun Morgan and I were having. My insides warmed as I pictured him behind the bar.

My song wobbled to an end, guilt cutting it short. I hadn't done anything wrong last night, but my dreams were borderline betrayal. Yes, they were only dreams, but the way my body ignited just before I woke was a testament to my desire. I couldn't think of Cole that way. I was with

David...and I loved him. He deserved my loyalty.

And so of course my thoughts flicked straight to shower man. I rolled my eyes.

David! Think of David!

But I couldn't.

I'd tried to push shower man from my mind, avoiding showering around the same time, just in case he reappeared. I'd really had to resist the urge to find him again. To hear that voice one more time would have been magical.

My blood sizzled as I imagined him, his deep voice floating over the shower wall. I closed my eyes, feeling guilty for trying to picture another naked man when I heard it.

The deep voice oozed into my shower stall. At first I thought it was just my imagination. I jerked still, my heading tipping to the side to listen, and there it was again.

He was singing "I Wanna Know Your Name" by The Intruders...and he was singing it to me.

I drew in a breath, my belly coiling tight with desire. Turning off the spray, I leaned my head against the tiles so I could hear him better. His smooth, chocolate voice drifted around me. I could dive into that sound and swim there all day. Heat rushed between my legs, and I had to press my fingers into the wall to keep myself standing. His rich voice faded out as the song came to an end, replaced by a request that made my eyes snap open.

"I want to meet you. Wait for me outside."

"No." The word fired out of my mouth.

"What?"

"I—I can't."

David. I rubbed my tummy, trying to expel the fire, stepping out of the shower and reaching for my towel. I had to get out of there.

"Why not?" I couldn't tell if the muffled voice

was sad or annoyed.

Throwing my shirt on, I struggled to pull it down over my damp skin. "I'm sorry," I softly called to him. "I have a boyfriend...who I really love. I can't. I can't meet you."

Pressing my lips together, I closed my eyes.

Desire was playing tug-of-war with logic and doing its damnedest to win. Trying to struggle into my leather pants would have been near impossible, so I wrapped the towel around my waist and grabbed my stuff.

"At least tell me your name," I heard him call.

Closing my eyes, I bunched my lips and tiptoed out of the room.

"Are you still there?"

Hating myself, but knowing it was the right thing to do, I swung the bathroom door open and raced down the empty hallway.

FIFTEEN
COLE

I called out to her three more times before giving up and slamming off the shower. Slumping down on the wooden bench just outside the stall, I didn't even care that I was naked. Water ran down my limbs like long, slow tears.

She'd said no.

Biting the inside of my cheek, I banged my head against the wall behind me.

I should have grabbed my stuff and chased her the second I thought she'd left, but then what? Force her to break up with her boyfriend? I didn't even know the woman. She was obviously loyal.

My voice clearly didn't impact her the way hers did me.

I sighed.

Hearing her sing "Someone To Watch Over Me" nearly made me cry. That in itself was unnerving. I didn't cry. I hadn't cried since watching my parents' caskets being lowered into the ground. I'd wiped away those final tears and sworn to never feel anything again.

This year was screwing with me big time. Damn girls. They messed up everything. Why'd they have to be taken already? I couldn't have Ella because she was with David, and now I couldn't have my songbird because she was taken, too. Had I missed the boat? I was only twenty-one, for fuck's sake.

Pressing my elbows into my knees, I grabbed two clumps of wet hair and stared at the bathroom floor.

She'd said no.

Why did it have to hurt so damn much?

She was supposed to be my way past Ella. She was supposed to solve all my problems, but she didn't want me.

"We don't want him."

My mind flashed with the words that had laid the initial bricks around my heart.

"Mr. and Mrs. Reynolds, we understand that you are heartbroken over the death of your son, but your grandson needs you," the social worker said.

"We are far too elderly to care for a ten-year-old boy. What could we possibly offer him? We've finally secured a place in a retirement village we've been wanting for months. They won't allow us to have it if we bring a child with us." Grandma Pauline turned to look at me. "Honey, it's not that we don't love you. We're thinking of your best interests. You don't want to live with two old fuddy-duddies like us."

I wanted to spit at her sweet smile, but instead

turned my head away. I caught the social worker's sympathetic look as my eyes traveled to the window. He let out a reluctant sigh and tried one last time.

"You are aware that if you refuse to take him, he'll become a ward of the state. He'll go into foster care."

"Yes, we've thought this through. Foster parents will be able to provide him with a life we can't. It's for the best. Now, where do we sign?"

I closed my eyes, my insides turning numb as I listened to the scratch of pen on paper.

I squeezed my eyes tight and stood tall, yanking my towel off the hook. Roughly drying my body, I got dressed in sharp, snappy movements that nearly ripped my clothes.

People didn't want me. That just seemed to be the way my life went.

The only people who had ever kept me around were Nina and Malachi. They were the exception to the rule. The only exception.

This was why I didn't want a girl. They just complicated everything. Light and casual. That was the way to avoid the hurt. It was that simple.

I had far more important things to focus on than being in a relationship. Nina was full of crap. Having a partner wouldn't make anything better; it would just be a let-down.

I needed to get my head out of the loved-up clouds and back into reality.

Study.

Work.

My dreams of the pub.

"That's all you should be thinking about," I muttered.

SIXTEEN
ELLA

Guilt.

It felt like a chain around my neck, pulling me down and dragging me through a muddy river. I deserved it. I was fantasizing about two different men when I should only have one on my mind.

The one. David. My one.

I repeated the word *one* through my head as I scurried down the hall with my bundle of clothes. Bypassing my room, I walked straight to David's, not even bothering to knock. It was unlocked and all seemed quiet when I entered. Cole's door was open, his bed empty. I closed my eyes with relief. He'd obviously spent the night at the pub. I thought I'd heard him say he might.

Pulling in a breath, I tried to quell the fire still

racing through my body. I was hot, for all the wrong reasons. I needed to vanquish these thoughts from my head and focus.

Gently turning the handle, I pushed David's door open and crept in. The room was starting to grow light. I could just make out David's scruffy locks of sandy-blond hair on the pillow. I grinned as I watched him moan and roll over.

His eyes squinted and popped open when I clicked the door shut.

"Hey," I whispered.

"Hey, baby," he mumbled, rubbing his eyes. "What are you doing here?"

I shrugged and simpered. "I missed you." Biting my lower lip, I swallowed and dropped my clothes to the floor. Tugging on my towel, I let it fall and enjoyed the slow smile creeping over his face as I wriggled out of my T-shirt.

Standing naked in front of him felt good, like somehow I was doing the right thing. Showing him I loved him would cleanse me of my guilt.

He threw back the cover with a chuckle and I slipped beneath the sheets. His hands traveled up my torso, squeezing my breast as his lips hit my neck, nipping and sucking my soft skin. With my body already sizzling thanks to shower man, it didn't take much. I cried out in ecstasy, squeezing David's neck and scraping my fingers down his back.

Helping David rip off his shirt, I slathered his neck in warm kisses while he touched me, making me reach climax in record time.

I shifted beneath him, keeping my eyes closed as he kissed my lips and plunged inside of me. It felt good, euphoric, heated...like the best sex we'd ever had. Gripping his shoulders, I moved to his rhythm, panting softly as our bodies slapped together.

"Oh, Ella!"

I squeezed my eyes shut even tighter, hearing a different voice call my name. A voice that set my insides alight. Liquid fire coursed through my veins as I lost myself in the moment. A moment that had nothing to do with David.

He finished quickly after that, arching his back before slumping on top of me with a luxurious sigh.

"Wow," he murmured, nibbling at my neck. "Wow, Ella, that was amazing."

"Yeah," I whispered, my voice quivering. I pressed my lips into his shoulder, trying to enjoy the taste of his hot skin.

But it didn't work.

Now I felt worse.

Coming to see David had been a huge mistake.

Slipping out of me, he rolled me onto my side and collected me against him. His lips skimmed the back of my shoulders and he chuckled. "You know I usually hate surprises, but surprises like this...feel free to bring those around anytime."

I laughed with him, trying to sound jolly and playful when all I wanted to do was cry.

Leaning over me, he squashed me into the bed as he reached for his watch. "This early morning wake-up call was a big help, Ella. I have a huge day ahead, but you know..." He rolled me onto my back and settled between my legs again. "I can probably finish early tonight...take you out to dinner." He kissed my nose. "Maybe after that we could come back for a little more..." He wiggled his eyebrows and I had to concentrate on smiling.

"Whatever works for you."

His eyes lit with a smile as he leaned down to kiss me. I closed my eyes and tried to focus on the feel of his tongue, the warm taste of it. It had always been such a comfort, given me a sense of security, but right now it felt wrong, and there was only one reason why.

David and I had been sleeping together for just over a year and not once had we had sex this hot. It made me sick to think the only reason was because I'd been thinking of somebody else...a mystery man whose voice gave me fever.

SEVENTEEN

COLE

I shouldered my door open, still antsy and frustrated. I had no idea what I was going to do with my day. Nina and Mal didn't need me at the pub until after noon. It was going to be a long morning.

Shutting the door behind me, I heard muffled groans from behind David's door and wanted to slit my wrists.

"Oh, Ella!"

I closed my eyes as he called out her name.

Maybe a noose would be better.

Dumping my wet towel and dirty laundry into the hamper, I pressed my hands over my ears and made a beeline for the door. This morning was going to be painful enough without having to picture beautiful Ella writhing beneath my roommate.

I pulled the door back quickly and stormed out of the room, shoving my hands in my pockets and leaping down the stairs. I needed a long walk and some sunshine. A coffee wouldn't go amiss, either. I looked at my watch.

Six hours until I was due at work.

"Crap," I muttered, heading toward Hyde Park. Like hell I was going back to my room today. Images of those two having sex scalded my brain and I squeezed my eyes shut for a minute. Shaking my head, I opened them and nearly barreled straight into Morgan.

"Oh hey, sorry." I caught her arm before she fell.

She chuckled. "No problem."

Her dark eyes were sparkling, her cheeks flushed. She was still dressed in that black number of hers, her heels dangling from her fingers.

"Coming home from Brad's?"

She nodded, her flushed cheeks growing a shade darker.

Great, so I was the only person on the planet who hadn't had sex last night.

I pursed my lips and looked across the park.

"Hey, last night was awesome, by the way." Morgan patted my arm. "We had such a great time. I haven't seen Ella that happy in...I don't know if I ever have, actually."

"Yeah." I couldn't help a chuckle. "You two looked like you were having fun."

"It was nice to see Ella loosen up a bit. She's always so shy and closed off. She can be pretty insecure sometimes. I was surprised she even showed up. Her original plan was to get into her PJs and watch a movie."

I could see that. Images of her snuggled on the couch, cuddling a pillow, with her slender legs tucked beneath her made me smile. That wouldn't be a bad way to spend a night, especially if she was tucked up against me.

I drew in a sharp breath and focused back on Morgan. "Well good for her then."

"Yeah, that's what I thought too. I was proud of my little Ella." She lifted her chin and laughed.

"You know you sound like her mother sometimes."

Morgan shrugged. "Her and Jody, my little sister...we're really close, like family. We understand each other."

"I can see that."

Her serious look faded as she tipped her head and gazed at me.

"So, what are you doing out so early? I thought you'd be crashing after such a big night."

I wasn't sure how much to say, but Morgan seemed to know everything about Ella anyway, so I shrugged and went for the truth. "I just needed to get out of the room." I pointed back to the dorms. "There's a little bit of animal sex going on in there this morning."

Morgan's eyebrows quirked. "Really? David and...Ella?"

I frowned. "Why do you look so surprised?"

"No, it's just, I don't..." She shook her head. "When Ella talks about her and David, it just never sounds that passionate."

"Huh." I so didn't need to hear that. "Well, maybe she's not telling you everything."

"Yeah, maybe." Morgan's frown was still in place. She opened her mouth to speak then closed it, but then opened it again. "He's not cheating on her, is he?"

"Not unless the girl he's cheating with is also called Ella."

"Oh." Morgan's eyes rounded with

understanding. "Okay." She huffed out a laugh, looking relieved when all I felt was annoyance. I didn't want David to be a cheater, but it would be pretty damn convenient if he were.

My face bunched tight at the thought. I was such an asshole.

"Hey, are you okay?" Morgan rubbed my arm.

"Of course." I cleared my throat. "Just trying to figure out what I'll do with my morning."

"You know, my last roommate used to have really noisy sex. Do you remember Susanna? Short, black hair, nose ring?"

I shook my head, not recalling her immediately.

"Well anyway, she loved sex and was a real screamer." Morgan grimaced. "It was very painful and happened a lot. I couldn't spend that much time walking around campus, so I got into the habit of putting on my earphones and watching movies or listening to music really loud. I bought those awesome noise-canceling ones. I have a spare pair if you'd like to borrow them."

"That's not a bad idea." I snickered. "I want to be prepared for next time." I raised my eyebrows and we both chuckled.

"Well, swing by anytime to collect them."

"Thanks, Morgan." I gave her a soft smile. I got why Ella loved her so much; she was a cool chick.

I turned to watch her leave, the fleeting thought that maybe she was my shower diva firing through my head. I scoffed at myself and turned away. I was freaking obsessed.

"Get over yourself, Reynolds," I whispered between clenched teeth. "Enough now, you fool."

Stomping over the grass, I pushed aside all thoughts of female creatures, instead trying to work through my business plans and how I was going to make my pub as brilliant as Quigg's.

EIGHTEEN

ELLA

I cut into my fish, pressing a small dollop of creamy risotto over the mouthful before consuming it. It tasted divine. I closed my eyes and relished the flavors exploding in my mouth.

"You like it, huh?"

"Yeah, it's amazing." My eyes rounded as I looked across the table at David. He was going all out to impress me. No doubt an attempt to make up for being so busy this weekend, or maybe he was still running high after our early-morning quickie.

I glanced around the hotel restaurant. Strains of piano music wafted in from the lobby, combining with the quiet murmur of mealtime conversation. It was really nice.

Nice.

Not fun, energetic, lively.

Nice.

I took a sip of my water, trying to convince myself that I was having as much fun here as I had been at Quigg's.

I was.

This was classy and enjoyable. I didn't need to be up shaking my ass in order to have fun.

"So, I had a really good day. Our study group got through so much." David piled his fork high and chewed around his words. "We spent the afternoon testing each other. Guess how well I did."

His eyes were dancing.

"One hundred percent." I grinned.

"Well, nearly. I got one question wrong, so I want to rework that section tomorrow."

I nodded, forcing a smile. Placing my glass down, I forgot my food for a moment. "You don't worry that you're working too hard, do you?"

"Ella, there's no such thing as working too hard," he sniggered. "If I want to get ahead, I have to earn it."

"Yeah, but what about fun? Re-energizing with a little R and R."

"I have fun." He lifted his fork full of food. "I'm having fun right now." He leaned toward me. "I had fun this morning."

I breathed out a laugh that sounded so incredibly fake to me. He didn't seem to notice.

"And there'll be more fun coming." He winked.

"What do you mean?" I tipped my head.

"Well, I've decided to take Mom's advice and have two twenty-first birthday parties."

I raised my eyebrows.

"Yeah." He grinned. "Since Luke can't make it home for Christmas, he's going to fly here for my college twenty-first party and then we can celebrate a family twenty-first in December."

"Cool." I nodded. "What are you thinking of doing?"

"Well, Luke's friends with the hotel manager at Hudson's. You know, that swanky place uptown?"

I didn't, but nodded anyway; it was just easier.

"He's booking a room for me, and we'll have a nice dinner with some champagne and cocktails. I'll invite all my UChicago friends. We'll have one or two speeches, and then I'll cut a cake, I guess."

"Nice."

There was that word again.

Smoothing down my dress and rearranging my napkin, I let David's voice wash over me as he continued chatting. The conversation inevitably moved from party plans back to his awesome day. He was on fire, excited about the test on Monday. I didn't think that emotion was even possible when talking about tests of any kind.

I smiled and nodded like I always did when he chatted about this stuff. He was so enthusiastic and animated, it was easy to watch him. He was going to do so great with his life. He had it all mapped out, and I was part of that plan.

It might not be exciting, but it felt secure and comfortable, which was a good thing.

"Will you call me when you get there?" I clung to his shoulders.

The bustle of LAX blurred around me as I tried to make the moment last.

"Of course, baby." He pulled away from me, holding me at arm's length. "You'll be by my side in no time."

"There's no guarantee I'll even get in to UChicago next year."

"Well, if you don't, we'll try for the year after that."

I smiled at him. I loved the way he always sounded so

confident, so sure.

"I've got a plan, Ella, and you're part of that plan, so no matter what, we're gonna make this work."

He kissed me hard, sealing all his promises between our locked lips.

I'd believed him, waved him off with high hopes and clung to that promise ever since.

David was my security; everything I needed in life was wrapped up in his confidence...his plan. Chewing down my last piece of fish, I washed it away with lemon water and dabbed my lips with the thick, cloth napkin.

Being with David was the right move for me. Shower guy got me hot and Cole made my mouth water, but what would they ever provide for me? I had a life and a future with David.

So, why did that thought not thrill me the way it used to?

I placed my napkin on the table with a little frown, muttering a thank you to the waiter as he collected my plate.

"Do you want any dessert?"

I shook my head. I felt a little off, and I wasn't sure if it was the food or the myriad of doubts attacking me.

The check arrived and David gave it a once-over like he always did, making sure all the details were accurate. Satisfied, he calculated a fair tip and paid accordingly.

He thanked the waiter, giving him a confident smile and turned back to me, sliding his hand across the table and over my fingers. He squeezed my wrist, his dimple appearing.

"I can't have you staying the night, because I really need to get some decent sleep for tomorrow, but do you want to end your evening in my bed?"

No.

That was my first thought.

No?

What the hell was wrong with me?

Pushing a grin over my lips, I nodded. "Of course."

"What would I do without you, Ella? I'm the luckiest guy on this earth."

Swallowing down my doubts, I relished the smile he shone me and rose from the table. How could I not want to be with a guy who said things like that to me?

His fingers wove between mine and we walked out of the restaurant. David hailed a taxi quickly and pulled me into his arms, kissing my hair and squeezing me to him.

He no doubt spent the taxi ride thinking about how sweet his life was, while I spent it trying to psych myself up for a sexual encounter that had my mind focused on one man and not three.

*****

"What's the matter?" David pushed back on his arms, peering down at me through the darkness.

"What?" I rubbed my hands up his bare sides, knowing the answer, but never daring to say it.

"You just didn't seem into it."

"I was." Not really, because I spent most of that intimate tryst trying not to imagine someone else inside me; a faceless man with a voice that did me in. "I'm sorry, I just feel a little off. My tummy is..."

David let out a sigh. "The wheat thing again?"

"Yeah, I think so." It was actually starting to hurt, and I had a sinking feeling the next day was going to suck.

David slipped out of me, rolling onto his back and resting his arm on his forehead. "I thought you chose carefully. You need to ask and stop assuming that what you order will be gluten-free."

There was an edge of annoyance in his softly-spoken words. I couldn't help wondering if it was more to do with the fact we hadn't just repeated our passionate encounter from this morning or the fact I hadn't been more careful with my menu choice.

"I'm sorry. I didn't see anything in my meal that could have had wheat...unless the fish was coated in flour or something," I mumbled. Damn it. It would have been that.

My stomach constricted in protest, confirming my suspicions.

I tried not to hunch over. David really hated it when I was careless on the wheat thing. Being a celiac was so annoying, and I tried really hard to never let it affect anyone around me.

In spite of his annoyance, his hand softly skimmed my belly. "You need to be more careful. I should have made you ask when you ordered."

"I'll try to be more assertive next time."

He flashed me an adoring grin and kissed my forehead before flopping back down beside me. "Ella Simmons. Assertive." He shook his head with a chuckle. "Those words don't go together, baby."

His laughter was sweet and teasing, but it still pissed me off. I hated my timidity. I wanted to be more assertive; I just didn't know how. I think David liked stepping up and playing hero, so he was more than happy to keep me as his quiet, mousy girl.

If truth be told, I preferred it that way, but for the first time ever I had to question if it was actually good for me.

I sat up, reaching for my underwear. "I'm pretty tired from last night. Maybe I should go."

"What'd you do last night?" David propped himself up on his elbow.

"I went out with Morgan and Brad. Well, I met them at Quigg's, anyway."

"Quigg's?" David flicked on the lamp. A dimple scored his cheek as he grinned at me, a little confused. "But Cole told me Chaos was playing there last night."

"Yeah, that's why Morgan invited me."

"But..." David snickered. "We hate loud bands like that."

I reached for my shirt, keeping my eyes downcast as I buttoned it up. "I don't mind them...sometimes. They were really good." Glancing up, I straightened my shirt and tried not to let David's look bother me. "What? You listen to techno. That can be loud."

"Yeah, but only in the car. I'd never go to a concert."

"This wasn't a concert. It was just a band playing in a bar." I huffed. "Am I not allowed to like loud, rock bands?"

"No, of course not." He reached for my hand. "I'm just surprised."

I met his smile with one of my own, knowing that his surprise was my fault. I shrugged. "I know you're not into that kind of stuff, and I'm just as happy going to the movies with you or a nice, quiet dinner."

"I love that we're into the same things...mostly." He chuckled, but I know my revelation unnerved him.

Perching on the edge of the bed, I ran my hand up his arm. "It's okay for us to like different stuff too, though, isn't it?"

"Yeah." He nodded. "Just don't ask me to ever go to Quigg's on a Friday night, okay?"

"Okay." I swallowed and looked away.

"I know I sound like an old man, but I know what I like, and I don't see any reason to put myself in a situation I won't enjoy, you know what I mean?"

"I know exactly what you mean." My forced smile hurt as I leaned toward him for a kiss.

He let out a pleasant moan then pulled back and gently held my neck. "I love you, baby. You make me so happy."

I grinned, my heart turned to mush by the look in his eye.

"Sleep well. Give me a call tomorrow afternoon, when you're done."

"Sounds good." He kissed me again before flopping back onto his pillow to watch me leave.

I waved and closed the door behind me, walking back to my room in a heavy silence. It weighed me down, making me feel small and pathetic. I couldn't help a touch of resentment.

I did stuff for David all the time: sat through his boring chatter about his study group, listened to his endless assignment work and his plans for our future. I went to all his debate meets at high school...and he didn't even take me to his senior prom. Instead, we went out for a quiet, romantic dinner, but...

I tutted. This was my fault. I'd never put up a fight when he'd suggested we skip prom and do something different. I was always happy to just go along with whatever he wanted. I wasn't afraid to upset him...I didn't think; I just wanted to make him happy. He took such good care of me that first year we were together, I felt like I owed him.

His confidence made me feel stronger, secure. I clung to that when he was away from me, learning to stand on my own two feet a little, knowing he was over here setting up our future. It seemed to drive me...until crunch time when I actually had to leave my comfort zone and follow him.

Now that I was here and with him again, it felt

different. I still loved him, no question, but something inside me was changing, and I couldn't decide if that was a good thing or not.

Reaching my room, I placed my hand on the knob and grimaced. My stomach clenched with pain, and I bit back my whimper as I entered the room. I hated my gluten allergy. It could be so debilitating.

I also hated my allergy to telling David the truth, which for the first time felt just as crippling.

Leaning against the back of the door, I looked to the ceiling, my eyes glassing over with tears.

I felt like I was stuck in quicksand; a sweet quicksand that was pleasant and secure, but a quicksand nonetheless. I couldn't break David's heart. He loved me. I made him happy.

That was enough, right?

NINETEEN

COLE

I woke the next morning, restless and agitated. Saturday had been a crappy day walking around campus, trying to avoid my room in case Ella and David were at it again. After three hours of mindless wandering, I couldn't take it anymore and braved my place. It had been mercifully empty, so I slumped on the couch watching a movie and trying to tune out.

Quigg's was once again busy but not as much fun. I got home just after midnight. The place appeared quiet and still, David's door closed. I had no idea if Ella was in there or not, but just the idea made sleeping near impossible.

After a quick, silent shower with no sweet songbird to accompany me, I headed back to my room and dumped my stuff. David's door remained shut, and I didn't want to kick around and wait for the sounds of soft moaning again.

Damn. Another long day.

Nina and Malachi told me to take today off. They opened later on a Sunday, and they could cover the lunch rush without me. Nina would no doubt tell me off if I showed up.

"Get your butt back to school and study," she'd say.

That was the last thing I felt like doing.

Rubbing the back of my neck, I looked across at David's door and mumbled, "First things first."

I knew it was only eight, but Morgan seemed like an early riser, and I figured Ella was already in David's bed, so it wasn't like I'd be waking her. I needed those headphones.

Brushing past a few students, I made my way to room 309 and gently tapped on the door.

A minute later it crept open, and I faced a pale-looking Ella. She clutched the door, slightly hunched over. She squinted at me as if she was trying to hide some pain in her body.

I wanted to ask her if she was all right, but didn't know if she'd find that too intrusive.

"Hey." I smiled instead.

"Hi, Cole." She leaned her head against the door. "What's up?"

"I was just wondering if Morgan was here."

Her thin eyebrows bunched together.

"She was going to lend me some headphones." I didn't know why I felt a need to justify seeing Morgan.

"Oh, she's not here right now, but I can go and look for them if you like."

She winced and her knuckles grew white as she gripped the wood. She looked ready to double over.

"Are you okay?" I reached out for her, worry coursing through me.

"Just a tummy ache." She whimpered.

"It looks like more than a tummy ache. Do you need me to...call David or take you to the doctor?"

"No." She rubbed her forehead. "It's...I get this sometimes." She squeezed her eyes shut. "I'm allergic to gluten...wheat...and I think...I *know*...I accidentally had some last night. The fish, it's the only thing I can think of. It must have been coated in flour before they fried it. It didn't even occur to me when I was ordering it." She scrunched over for a second, clutching her belly. "It only lasts for a day. I just have to drink a ton of water and take it easy. Compared to some, this is mild."

"This is mild?"

She looked so miserable, and I was helpless to do anything about it. I hated that.

"Where's David? Do you want me to go and get him?"

"No, he's studying. I don't want to bother him. He needs to focus, and I just need to take it easy for the day. There's nothing he can really do to help me." Her soft voice was frail. "Let me go and find those headphones for you."

"Don't worry about it." I waved my hand. "I can come back another time."

"Okay." Her large eyes glassed over as they hit me. Pressing her lips together, she looked like she was holding back the tears. I knew the second I left, they'd fall, and I just couldn't let that happen.

"Can I get you anything? What do you want most when you feel this way?"

"My mom." Her face crumpled and she closed her eyes, trying to pull herself together.

I swear my heart was going to crack watching her. I couldn't stop myself from gently asking, "Can I come in?"

Her large eyes hit me again, punching through my chest and melting me. Without a word, she pulled the door a little wider and stepped aside. I closed the door behind me, shoving my hands into my pockets and giving her a sympathetic smile. Wrapping her arms around herself, she walked back to the couch and flopped onto it, curling into a ball.

I noticed her empty glass and quietly collected it, going to the mini-fridge and finding a half-empty water bottle. She sniffed as I walked the refilled glass back to her and placed it on the coffee table.

"Thanks," she murmured.

I pulled the blanket so it covered her feet and sat down on the edge of the couch. Her toes brushed against my thigh, but she didn't move them. She looked like she had a pretty sweet headache to go along with her tummy pain. Her shaky fingers continued to rub just above her right eyebrow.

"Are you sure you don't want me to call David?"

"No, he's studying, and you know him; he's terrible with sick people. When he's sick, he just likes to go into his little man-cave and pretend the world doesn't exist."

I chuckled, remembering his bout of the flu last year. He was like a grumpy bear.

Fingering the tassels on Ella's blanket, I gave her a small smile. "Let me guess: you, on the other hand, need a little TLC."

She grinned. "I know. I'm so pathetic."

"No, you're not." I patted her leg. "Do you want me to grab your computer? We could set you up on Skype with your mom."

Her face washed with a heart-crushing sadness, her eyes glossing over once more. "I'm surprised David hasn't told you."

I swallowed. He hadn't, and I had a sinking feeling I knew what she was about to tell me. Her mother was dead.

"My parents passed away a few years ago."

My stomach did a belly flop. She was an orphan? Like me?

Her lips pursed to the side as she brushed away a tear. "Most of the time, I'm okay. It's just some days...I don't know. Mom was always perfect when I was sick. I miss her fussing, and her cold hand on my forehead." Ella's voice wobbled. "She'd rub my back, and we'd sit on the couch together watching *Dirty Dancing* and *The Notebook*." She sniffed and softly chuckled.

My heart constricted. "How old were you when they died?"

"Fifteen."

"I'm so sorry, Ella." My eyebrows moved as I said the words, total understanding running through me.

She paused, turning her head to study me. Her eyes narrowed. "You sound like you mean it."

"I do."

"No." She sat up, perching her weight on her elbow. "I mean, you sound like you know what it's like."

I looked away with a soft sigh. "I do."

"How'd they die?"

"Car accident." I cleared my throat the way I always did after saying those words.

Her soft lips parted, surprise flicking through her expression. "Mine too," she whispered.

My breath hitched and our eyes locked for an intense moment of something I'd never experienced before. I couldn't even label it. There was just this powerful awareness flowing between us.

She finally looked away with a sad smile,

pulling one of the blanket tassels straight. "The worst memory of my life was opening up that door to two police officers with pale faces and sad eyes. I just knew the second I saw them..." She licked her bottom lip. "Mom and Dad weren't coming home from their dance class. In fact, they'd never be coming home again."

"Yeah. It's weird how you know. You just get that feeling." I never talked about this with anyone, but I felt like it was only fair after what she'd just told me. Besides, she got it. I mean she actually got it. "I was at summer camp and..." I chuckled and then winced. "Actually, I was getting kicked out of summer camp for putting cherry bombs in the toilets."

Her eyes rounded and she giggled, before nestling back onto her pillow and shifting her body so she could look at me.

"I was just experimenting. I didn't even know if they would work or not."

"But they did." Her laughter grew.

I nodded with a bashful smile. "Yep, they definitely did." I clicked my tongue. "The director was so pissed, he kicked me out that day." The humor vanished from my tone, sucked into a morbid vortex. "Mom and Dad were coming to pick me up and I was really nervous. I knew they'd be disappointed, and I hated letting them down. Although, I was kinda hoping Dad would find it funny." My wide-eyed stare went fuzzy, my voice dropping to a near whisper. "The longer it took them to get there the more nervous I got, and then it finally started to sink in. They weren't coming. When the director came through to tell me, I already knew."

"It's like your innards are being crushed to dust, right?" Ella's voice and tone matched mine. "I thought I'd never be able to breathe normally again."

"Yeah. Me too." I looked at her. "I was ten when it happened, and I think I stopped talking for a few months. I just couldn't think past the numb."

"Do you have any siblings?"

"Nah, it was just me."

"Such a lonely feeling, isn't it."

"I'm guessing you're the same."

"Yep." She nodded. "Who'd they send you to?"

I shrugged, trying to put on the tough veneer I always did. She was making it damn hard to hold it in place though. "My grandparents didn't want me— they said they were too old, so I went into foster care."

"Sucked?"

"Definitely; well, until I got to Nina and Mal's. I hadn't lasted more than six months in a place before them, and they had me all the way through high school. I work for them now, actually."

"Quigg's?"

"Yeah."

"That's really cool."

"I know. I'm one of the lucky ones, right?"

"Yeah. I guess." Her shoulder popped up with a shrug. "I got sent to live with my crazy aunt. She's really weird and her people skills are basically non-existent. I mean, I feel like she cares about me because I'm her dead sister's kid, but she doesn't like me living there. I spent most of my high school years sleeping over at Morgan and Jody's place."

"You girls do seem ridiculously close."

"We're family. I don't think I could have survived without them...or David." Her gaze fluttered away from mine. "We got together after Morgan left for college. Jody was going through this rebellious phase, and he really helped me through, you know."

"Yeah, he's a good guy." I looked across the

room, trying to ignore the feel of her feet pressed against my thigh. Maybe staying was a really bad idea. I popped a glance at her. She was staring at the frozen TV screen, looking sad and fragile.

I couldn't leave her; not just because it felt mean, but because I didn't think I could make myself move. "So, what are you watching?" I cleared my throat, trying to sound upbeat.

"*Dirty Dancing*." She bit her lip, her smile bashful.

"No one puts Baby in a corner, right?"

She giggled, the sound melodic and beautiful. I grabbed the remote and pressed play, nestling back into the couch and getting comfy.

I wasn't doing anything wrong, just sitting with a girl who needed a little looking after. Too bad it felt so freaking amazing. My eyes shifted back to her cute face, nestled against the pillow. She quietly mouthed the words to the movie, making me smile. Crossing my arms, I pressed my palm into my chest. My heart was pounding, elated with this moment and our perfect, heartfelt conversation. I could so easily get addicted to this. David was the luckiest guy on earth.

TWENTY

ELLA

Watching *Dirty Dancing* with Cole was the best. I didn't know why it was better than any other time in particular, but I loved having him there. I kept sneaking glances at him, loving the way his lips twitched with a grin. His eyes were totally transfixed on the final dance...the best end to a movie ever.

As the credits rolled, he turned my way. "You know, when my mom used to watch this, she'd always rewind the end and watch the dance again."

"Well, it's *Dirty Dancing*, that's what you're supposed to do."

With a quiet chuckle, he reached for the remote and did just that. When Patrick Swayze walked into the room, Cole's head whipped toward me, his right eyebrow arching.

"No one puts Baby in the corner," he said in a deep voice.

A loud laugh exploded from my lips, giggles rippling through my body. They kind of hurt, but I couldn't help it. Cole was so easy to be around. I didn't like being around people I barely knew when I felt this sick, but Cole was so relaxed and easy to be with. The movie came to an end, and I pressed my lips together, resisting the urge to sing.

"So what other kinds of movies do you like?" Cole patted my leg.

I wanted him to rest his hand there; it felt like the natural thing to do, but he moved it, and I had to look away so he wouldn't spot my disappointment. "Everything. I love movies...except horror or any realistic torture or anything like that."

"A softie. I thought so." He winked at me.

"How about you?"

"Yep, love them. I'll watch anything. My dad was a total movie freak; he had the biggest collection of DVDs. We used to do Friday movie night...every Friday. Mom would make the popcorn, Dad and I would shift the living room around, put a big mattress on the floor with a ton of pillows. It was awesome." His voice grew soft and distant, and then he took in a deep breath and smiled at me. "It was one thing I really held on to. I was moved from one place to another and my best friends were my computer and Dad's massive box of DVDs. I just used to hide in my room and watch whenever I was home."

"I'm guessing that's a lot of screen time."

"Yeah, Nina put an end to that pretty quickly." He chuckled. "I hated her for it at first, but she told me she was doing it because she really cared about me. I remember screaming at her about family movie night and just going ballistic before storming out of the house."

"You ran away?"

"Yeah, but the cops brought me back that night. Found me sitting on a street corner. A fourteen-year-old little shit with attitude to burn."

My heart squeezed, imagining the pain he must have been going through.

"But..." Cole lightly slapped his knee. "That Friday when I got home from school, Nina was down in the bar setting up the chairs in rows. They were facing this big screen at the back of the room." He grinned. "For the next three years, Quigg's had a movie night every Friday, and I was allowed to pick the movie...every week."

My eyes were glistening when he turned to face me. His smile was broad and heartfelt.

"Those two saved my life, you know."

"Just like Morgan and Jody saved mine."

"I guess we are among the lucky, aren't we?"

"As far as orphans go, I suppose."

My melancholy comment dropped an awkward silence into the room that I had to remedy. Cole's distracting presence was the perfect antidote to my stomach pain, and I really didn't want him to go.

Sitting up, I nestled the pillow behind my back and hugged my knees to my chest. "Top Ten Friday night movies. Go."

His face lit with a smile, before he threw his head back. "I can only choose ten?"

I chuckled. "First ten you think of."

The next hour whittled away as we talked movies. His Top Ten was pretty awesome and I kept adding to it. It soon became a Top Twenty and then morphed into a Top Fifty. The conversation then veered toward TV and books. Laughter and teasing peppered our chatter, which occasionally grew soft with painful reminders from the past. Talking to him so openly was easy, because I knew he got it. I didn't delve into all my fears or anything, but I could sense he read between the lines when I told him a story or two. I certainly read his book and it told me a lot.

We both jumped when the door jiggled open, and I glanced at the clock. My eyes bulged. Cole had been here for hours.

Morgan stepped in and glanced our way, surprise flickering over her features before she pulled herself together.

"Hey." Her grin bounced from me to Cole. "You come to get those headphones?" She winked.

Cole blushed.

I frowned.

What was the deal with the headphones?

I shuffled back on the couch, moving away from Cole. I hadn't even noticed when I inched forward. We were practically in each other's laps.

Cole cleared his throat and rose off the cushions, pulling his shirt straight.

"Ah, yeah. Headphones would be great. Thanks, Morgan."

"Let me grab them for you." She dumped her purse and clipped into her room.

Cole wouldn't look at me while we waited. Instead he crossed his arms, visibly awkward. I felt the loss keenly, my stomach pains returning with force now that I wasn't distracted.

I grimaced, clutching my waist and hoping Cole wouldn't notice.

Morgan stepped back into the room and he jumped around the couch.

"Here you go." She held them out, along with a memory stick. "This is the mix I used to listen to." She laughed.

What were they talking about? I really wanted

to know but didn't want to ask. They looked like they were sharing some private joke. Envy spiked through me, making me scowl as I nibbled on my thumbnail.

Cole took the memory stick. "What's on there?"

"Just a mix of rockbands and stuff. A little Chili Peppers, some Def Leppard, White Stripes."

"Ah, old school."

"Yeah," she chuckled. "But there's also some Green Day, Simple Plan, Good Charlotte, Black Eyed Peas, a little Pitbull. It's a real mix."

"You've got pretty eclectic tastes."

Morgan grinned. "Yeah, I love all kinds of music."

I wanted to pipe up that I did too, but kept my lips sealed. I wanted Cole to think I was cool, and I hardly thought admitting my love affair with Ella Fitzgerald music was going to help. Morgan always teased me for being born in the wrong era, which was why I'd never told David how much I loved to sing jazz. No, the only person who'd ever heard me do that with confidence was my shower man, who I now had no chance with thanks to my quick dismissal yesterday morning...not that I wanted a chance with him.

Argh! This was so freaking confusing.

I ran my hands through my hair, trying to forget my shower buddy, but the scene before me was hardly a pleasant distraction. Watching Morgan and Cole chuckle over her taste in music stung. I hated that it did. I was so frickin' immature. This spike of jealousy was real, and it bothered the heck out of me.

I was with David. Hello!

How was it possible to like three different guys at the same time?

David. David. David. David.

I crossed my arms tight across my chest,

determined to squash my anarchic feelings into submission. This was ridiculous. I had a gorgeous boyfriend who loved me. I made him happy. He needed me...and that was a nice feeling.

Reaching for my phone, I checked the screen. Blank. He was obviously still working. Antsy for a distraction, I stood from the couch, intending to go to my room and read while Cole and Morgan giggled over music. I didn't have to sit here and watch them.

The blanket fell from my knees as I turned to grab my pillow and then my body betrayed me.

Pain seared through my middle, making me buckle over, dots flashing before my eyes. I squeezed my eyes against the fuzz. Oh crap!

"Ella." Morgan's hand was on my back in an instant. "Sweetie, what's wrong?"

A little whine squeaked from my throat.

"She ate some wheat last night," Cole said.

"Oh no." Morgan rubbed my back. "What do you need?"

I groaned. "The bathroom."

Stumbling past her, I used the couch as a crutch until I ran out of it. Cole's strong arm grabbed me, wrapping around my waist. This was so humiliating.

"I'm okay." I tried to stand and brush him off, but he wouldn't have it. His arm remained around me all the way down the hall. Morgan walked quietly behind us and I wanted to die.

One, because my stomach was protesting in loud, growling rumbles. Cole knew the second I got into that bathroom, my body was going to erupt, and it wasn't going to be pretty.

Two, his arm felt divine.

Cole swung the door open for me and stepped back.

"I'm good." I held out my hand when Morgan

tried to step in and guide me to a stall. I stumbled my way to the end of the row and shakily locked myself inside, only just making it.

Tears popped from my eyes as I pressed my elbows into my knees. I had to be more careful.

"Side salads, just stick with the side salads," I whimpered.

Resting my head in my hands, I let out a long, slow sigh and sniffed.

I had to be more careful, and this time, I wasn't thinking about food.

*****

I shuffled back to my room about twenty minutes later. My stomach felt like it'd been put through a blender. Closing the door behind me, I leaned against the wood and shut my eyes.

"You okay, hun?" Morgan looked up from her magazine, giving me a sympathetic smile.

"Is he gone?"

"Yeah, he left as soon as you did."

"Okay. Good." I nodded, hunching over and weakly making my way to the couch. I slumped onto it. Morgan's hand gently pushed my shoulder until my head was resting on her knee. I closed my eyes, enjoying the feel of her cool hand on my forehead.

When my eyes crept back open, I noticed that the TV was all cued up, the first shot from *The Notebook* paused on screen.

"I love you," I whispered.

"I know."

She grinned down at me and reached for the remote. Before pressing play, her dark eyes hit me. "You want to talk about Cole?"

"Why would I want to talk about Cole?" I shifted my head on her lap, honing in on the screen so I wouldn't have to look at her.

"Ella, he's a really nice guy who just spent most of the day looking after you."

I swallowed. "Yeah, he is a really good guy."

"And David's best friend." Morgan rubbed her hand over my tense shoulder.

"Which is why I don't want to talk about him."

"You know—"

"Press play, Morgan."

She paused. I could feel her gaze on me, but I refused to look away from the screen. After a beat too long, she finally huffed out a soft breath, and whispered, "Pressing play."

The music swelled as the camera spanned over a quiet estuary, the sun rising in the distance. I loved this movie. I loved that a couple who were destined to be together made it, in spite of everything stacked against them. It was like they were addicted to each other, pulled together by a force outside of themselves. I wondered what a love like that felt like.

It scared me to think that maybe I already knew.

TWENTY-ONE
COLE

Everything was now totally messed up.

After making my big decision to get over girls and focus on my business plan, I had to go and spend the day with Ella, who in spite of her obvious pain managed to laugh and talk to me all day. She'd been so easy to chat to, her animated eyes lighting when we spoke about movies. She was a total romantic; I could see that in her right away. Man, I'd love to show her just how romantic I could be.

But I couldn't.

Damn it. It was so frickin' unfair.

I ambled through Millennium Park, glancing at Cloud Gate as I walked by. I didn't stop at the huge, shiny kidney bean this time, but I couldn't help slowing my pace to admire it. It was pretty cool. Chicago had some awesome artwork displayed for the tourists. People gathered around it, gazing up at their warped reflections. I remembered doing that with Malachi one day. We'd laughed our asses off.

Shoving my hands into my jacket pockets, I kept walking. I had no particular destination this weekend; I just knew I wanted to get out. I wasn't due at Quigg's until this evening, and I didn't want to spend the day hanging around campus. Since Ella had arrived, David and I had hardly hung out at all, but that was my fault, not his. He kept inviting me to join them, but it was just too damn hard.

It had been a week since I'd sat by Ella's side and talked the day away. I wanted a repeat, but the opportunity had never presented itself and it probably shouldn't anyway. She wasn't mine and never would be; I just had to face it.

I had managed one quick phone call. I'd actually started with Morgan, checking in with her to see how Ella was doing. I'd spent most of Sunday night stressing about her and the pain flashing over her face as I helped her to the bathroom. Morgan told me she had been fine by the morning but gave me her number anyway. It took me until the afternoon to give Ella a call.

"Hello, Ella speaking." Her voice was like the pink frosting on a cupcake.

"Hey, it's um, Cole. I hope you don't mind. Morgan gave me your number."

Her pause made my stomach coil. *"No, that's—that's great. How are you?"*

I chuckled. *"Me? I'm fine. How are you?"*

Another pause. This time I could picture her cheeks heating with color as she bit her lower lip. *"I'm all good now. Thank you for yesterday. You made it much easier for me to get through."*

"Anytime. I had fun."

"Me too."

There was an awkward beat. I thought of a million ways to fill it, but instead pressed my lips together. "Well, I'm glad you're okay. You take care."

"You too. Thanks for calling, Cole."

Man, I loved my name on her lips.

"See you 'round, Ella."

But I hadn't. I hadn't seen her all week and no matter how badly I wanted to call her again, I couldn't.

With a scowl, I hunched my shoulders against the wind and pressed forward, considering the idea of stopping for lunch soon. I thought about heading to Quigg's to hang out with Frankie. I was very aware he was living alone with Nina and Malachi, and he'd probably enjoy a little younger company for the afternoon. We could have some chow and then chuck a baseball around, or he could beat my ass at that new PS3 game he got for his birthday. Strider or something?

I nodded, liking that idea and turning north. But I couldn't move forward, because a pretty little thing was standing in my line of sight.

A slow smile formed on my face as I changed direction and headed toward Ella. Her delicate fingers were pinching her chin as she looked at her phone and then back up, doing a slow spin.

"You look lost."

She jerked at my quiet statement and spun around with a chuckle. Rolling her eyes, she shook her head and let out a bashful snicker. "I am. My sense of direction really sucks."

She was so adorable. I wanted to wrap her in a hug. I knew how she felt against me now, having practically carried her to the bathroom. Man, I'd do anything to experience that again. Not the Ella-being-sick part, but the me-helping-her-when-she-needed-me, part. My protective instincts had been on overdrive and I kind of liked it.

I cleared my throat and looked at her phone. "Where are you trying to get to?"

She passed me the phone. "Some restaurant that David loves. It's Italian, I think? It's on..."

"Oh yeah, Guiddo's." I passed the phone back without really having to look at it. "He loves that place. Come on, I'll show you the way."

"Really? Are you sure?"

"Of course." I smiled down at her.

She shone me a ray of sunshine and slipped her phone back into her coat pocket. "Thank you. He's having lunch with Mitch and Charlene and invited me last minute."

Guiddo's wasn't far from Millennium Park, so I didn't hurry. I had been enjoying my ambling pace and with Ella beside me, I was enjoying it even more. The tension seemed to drain from her the second she saw me and I was glad for it; being lost did suck.

"It's not far from here, about a block away."

"Okay, so I was sort of close." She shrugged. "I was trying to save my pennies and use the bus instead of a taxi. I got off a couple of stops too early and then walked this way and just totally didn't know where I was."

"Don't worry about it. Chicago's a big city; it's easy to get lost here."

"You seem to know your way around."

"I've been living here a tad longer than you. Put me in the middle of L.A. and I'd be lost in two seconds."

She chuckled. "Put *me* in the middle of L.A. and I'd be lost in two seconds."

I loved the way she could tease herself, and I had to fight the urge to lean down and kiss her.

She let out a little whine. "I hate that I'm like this, but God just forgot to give me a compass when I was born."

I smiled down at her. "Let me guess, your mom used to tell you that, right?"

She blushed. "My dad. He was always coming up with stuff like that."

We fell into silence, and I wanted to slow my pace even more. Guiddo's wasn't far and I wasn't done. Although I should have been. Hell, I should probably have been walking her there as fast as I could.

"So, what are you planning on doing after you graduate?"

Her question caught me off-guard.

"I, um, have a few ideas." I shrugged. I didn't really discuss my future plans with anyone other than Nina and Malachi. There were too many dream-squashers out there, and I didn't want to be put off.

"What are they?" Ella's keen eyes were so endearing, I broke the rules and turned her left instead of walking straight ahead. I figured I could get away with walking the long way around the block. It'd buy me ten more minutes of her undivided attention, and with her whacky sense of direction…I felt confident she'd remain unaware of my sneaky ploy to spend more time with her.

"Well…" I ran my hand through my hair. "I, uh, am quite keen on opening up a pub, kinda like Quigg's, but on the South Side, so I can cater to the UChicago crowd."

Ella's eyes sparkled and her mouth dropped open. "That is such a cool idea. Will you have bands come and play?"

"Yeah." I nodded, her enthusiasm making my

insides tingle. "I really want it to be a place for indie bands to showcase their work."

"Music students would love you! You could make it a place for them to perform and buskers, you could have them coming in too, earning a few bucks. They'd love it." Her hands spread wide, her eyes continuing to dance.

"That's what I was thinking, and then students come and hang out there. It'd be like a watering hole for them."

"Cafe feel during the day, pub at night."

"Exactly."

"I love it."

I couldn't hide my astonishment. Her reaction to my idea was epic and made me wonder if I should have been telling more people...but not David. The guy was so practical, he'd tear holes through it in a second.

"Can you not mention anything to David?" I winced.

"Why? Because his practicality would have your amazing dream deflated within about two seconds?" She winked and then grimaced, dropping her gaze. "Sorry, I shouldn't have said that. The world needs practical people."

"Yes it does, but it also needs encouragers." I nudged her gently with my elbow.

She looked at me with a blushing smile that did my heart in.

"You know, I'm really glad I told you. I don't often talk about my future plans."

"I get that. It's hard to make dreams come true." She swallowed.

"What are your dreams?"

I studied her carefully as her nose scrunched and she bit her lip. A breath shot out of her mouth as she chuckled and shook her head. "I don't..." She shrugged. "David's got lots of great plans for us.

He wants to get his law degree and eventually open up a practice of his own. We'll get a nice house somewhere and have a family."

"Ye-ah," I said slowly. "But what do you want? I mean, what do you want to do with your life?"

She wouldn't look at me. Her eyes skimmed the street ahead as her mouth opened and closed. "I don't..." She sighed and finally looked up at me. "I'm studying literature. I guess I'll finish that up and maybe go into teaching or something until I become a mother." None of those things looked to thrill her, and I couldn't help a frown. "To be honest, I haven't given it much thought. I just tend to focus on one week at a time, not a year in advance, you know what I mean?" Her chuckle was forced.

"Huh." Her comments worried me. I knew they shouldn't. It was none of my business. David's goals were obviously driving her too, but...

I cleared my throat, unwilling to just let it rest. "Does any of that stuff excite you?"

She shrugged and gave a pitiful nod. I wasn't buying it.

"I just think it's really important to have something that drives you in life...something to look forward to. What kind of stuff makes you zing?"

"Makes me zing?" She tittered.

"Yeah, what makes you happy? Like, really happy. You know, like when your heart just wants to burst out of your chest and fly through the sky."

Her smile was soft, her gaze enchanted by my words. I locked eyes with her and time froze until her forehead wrinkled and she looked away from me.

"Oh, Guiddo's." She pointed across the street and I spotted David sitting at one of the front tables by the window.

I tried to hide the sadness swamping me and forced a smile, but she wasn't looking at me anyway. Clearing my throat yet again, I pressed the button on the traffic lights. "David is amazing at analyzing things. He's a smart guy. Maybe I should tell him about my plans."

"Oh definitely. Yeah, he is." Ella's gaze popped up and she nodded, pressing her lips together. "Once you have your business plan all set and as hole-proof as possible, you should run it by him." She smiled at me. "I'll back you up. I think it's awesome."

"Thank you."

Her beautiful eyes held me steady as we waited for the lights to change. I could have gazed down at her all day, but the little red man turned green and we were forced to cross.

David saw us coming and jumped from his seat, meeting us at the door.

"I was about to call you." He wrapped Ella in his arms and kissed her cheek. "Hey, man." He smiled at me over her shoulder. "Want to join us?"

I knew I should have probably refused and headed to Quigg's, but I didn't want to leave her. Instead I decided to torture myself by following them through the restaurant and pulling out a chair. David's hand rubbed Ella's back as she greeted David's friends, Mitch and Charlene, and then reached for a menu.

I watched her from the corner of my eye. A little frown flickered over her features as she scanned the contents. It wasn't an angry frown; it was more disappointment than anything and I wondered why. Scanning my own menu, I soon figured it out.

Pasta, pizza, bread, flour, wheat, gluten, gluten, gluten.

I shot her a sympathetic smile and she wrinkled her nose, shaking her head slightly.

After carrying her to the bathroom last Sunday, I'd gone back to my room a worried wreck. David hadn't been there, so I couldn't ask him about it. Instead, I'd spent a couple of hours researching the Internet and finding out about celiac disease. Man, it was pretty limiting when it came to the diet.

Italian was the worst, too. What the hell was she supposed to order here?

As if hearing my thoughts, the waitress arrived with her pen and pad.

David leaned forward, a pleasant smile on his lips. "Yeah, can we grab a couple of garlic breads to start, and then I'll have the bacon and mushroom carbonara. Baby, what do you want?"

"I'll take the Greek salad, please."

It bugged me the way David didn't even notice her forlorn expression when she ordered. I knew he couldn't let her diet dictate every time they ate. Ella would no doubt hate that, but if it were me, I'd have been looking up every place in Chicago that served gluten-free food and taking her there.

Why should she always be the one to compromise?

I hid my scowl behind my menu as I waited for my turn to speak. I didn't have a right to be annoyed. It was her life and she could choose to compromise as much as she wanted to. She just seemed to do it a lot...and that worried me.

TWENTY-TWO

ELLA

My salad arrived looking sad and pathetic next to David's amazing-smelling pasta. I turned away from it, giving Cole a secret smile as he pushed his bowl of fries a little closer to me. I nabbed one and shoved it in my mouth, feeling naughty. I didn't know why. I wasn't breaking any laws. It actually felt quite fun and mischievous to have an inside joke going with Cole.

David was oblivious anyway. He was in the throes of a discussion with Mitch, a fellow law student, about some suit to do with music copyright.

"It is total plagiarism. They can't do it."

"I agree, but you have to look at the other party's viewpoint."

I held my sigh in check, diving into my salad and waiting for the conversation to become more interesting.

Cole's words were gnawing away at me. I loved his dream for the pub. The very idea of being a part of something like that thrilled me and made me wish I had dreams of my own. But I didn't. I'd never really considered what I wanted, because David had always been the answer. I wanted him and therefore I wanted his dreams, but did I really? Law hardly pressed my buttons and although I did want a family one day, I now couldn't rid my brain of a 1950s housewife working her ass off in the kitchen while she looked after screaming toddlers and waited for her husband to get home from work.

What makes you happy?

I hated that question, because the answer should have been David. For the last three years, it had been and I despised the fact that the simple answer wasn't cutting it anymore.

Nothing in my life made my heart want to fly right out of my chest...but I did remember feeling that giddy excitement years ago. Another memory surfaced as my mind wandered back to my pubescent self, sitting at a round kitchen table.

"What are you smiling about, little miss?" Mom rubbed the back of my head as she walked past me. I was trying to do my homework but struggling with the big question.

"I'm just laughing at myself."

"Why's that?" Mom chuckled.

"Well, for homework, we're supposed to pick a career choice and then research how to make that happen."

"So, what's the problem?"

I giggled. "I can't decide what I want to do. I've narrowed it down to architect or interior designer or a chef, but I also think a movie producer would be pretty cool...although probably an impossible career choice. I know it's only for homework, but I find it funny, and a little bit annoying, that I want to do so many things with my life. I'm not the kid who can say, 'I want to be this when I grow up,' because there are just so many cool options out there."

She smiled at me. "You don't have to settle on one thing. Plenty of people have multiple careers. I'm surprised singing diva isn't on your list."

I grinned and then shook my head. "Singing in public? Forget about it."

Mom chuckled. "I know what you mean, but I think you'd be good."

"I could do back-up singer maybe, but never front and center."

"You'll be amazing...at whatever you choose to do."

With a blush, I shook my head. "You know, I kind of feel like it doesn't even matter what my job is. I know it's important to love your work and stuff, but to me, the most important thing is the end of my day. I want to come from whatever I'm doing and walk into a house that's full of love and laughter. I want to be with someone I can sing and dance with, someone who'll make me laugh and love me no matter how crazy I am."

Mom's head tipped to the side, her eyes lighting with a mixture of pride and interest. "I like that you have your priorities straight." She slipped into the chair beside mine.

"I want to be like you and Dad. I want to show my kids what it's like to live in a house of love. That's possible, right? I can get that, can't I?"

Mom's eyebrows rose and she blinked at her tears. "Life isn't always roses and cupcakes," she whispered, reaching for my hand. "But my hope for you is that you'll meet your Prince Charming, and he'll dance you into the sunset and give you your happily ever after."

I grinned.

"Thanks, Mom." I squeezed her hand and nodded. "I love you."

"I love you too, sweetness."

The memory turned to ash in my mind. I'd never hear her say that to me again, and it hurt every time.

She was right. Life wasn't always roses and cupcakes; sometimes it was arsenic and manure.

Dreams could be stolen in the blink of an eye. Mine were snatched from me, and I'd pretty much been too afraid to dream since then. It wasn't until David came along that I found the courage to imagine past tomorrow. I could picture myself so clearly by David's side, supporting him, being the wife he wanted me to be. That image used to bring me so much comfort. He might not dance or sing, but he was charming. I had someone. I wasn't alone, and that was ultimately what I wanted. But as I sat there chewing on my rabbit food, I felt nothing but turmoil.

I looked up from my salad to watch Mitch's girlfriend, Charlene. She seemed right into the copyright conversation and was making intelligent comments, using terminology I didn't really know. She was a business major but obviously took a more vested interest in Mitch's study. I suddenly felt bad that I didn't do that with David and tried to catch up with what they were saying.

"Well, at least it wasn't some hideous song like, um, what's it called? I'm gonna be the man..." Charlene clicked her fingers. "500 Miles. You know, by the Proclaimers."

She made a gagging sound, and the three of them cracked up laughing.

"I love that song." I shrugged, spearing a piece of lettuce with my fork.

"What?" Charlene scrunched her nose with a

groan. "It's so incredibly painful."

About now, I'd usually back away from the conversation, mutter something about agreeing to differ and go back to munching my greens, but I just didn't feel like it today. I didn't know whether it was Cole's kick-ass business idea or my distant memories of dreaming that had me fired up, but for some reason, I decided to stand up for one of my favorite songs.

"I think it's beautiful. If you listen to the lyrics...it's one of the most romantic songs I know." There was no way on earth I'd sing it to these guys, but I knew the lyrics by heart. "I would walk 500 miles and I would walk 500 more, just to be the man who walked a 1000 miles to fall down at your door?" I glanced around the table. The only one with a gleam in his eye was Cole, and it encouraged me to finish my argument. "How can you not love that? If a guy ever sang that to me, I'd be putty in his hands."

Mitch chuckled, flicking his hand at David. "Looks like you'll need to start taking singing lessons, bro."

"Not on your life." David shook his head. "Ella knows I hate singing." He kissed my cheek. "I have other ways of wooing my girl." His eyebrows wriggled and I was forced to smile.

The truth was, he had wooed me. It hadn't taken much in high school; I had been a lost wreck, but he'd kept me steady. We'd lived apart for two years and I'd remained loyal and true. I hadn't wavered...until the morning after I arrived here and heard a voice in the shower.

I felt instant guilt and looked back to my salad.

"I like it too." Cole sat forward in his chair. "I agree with Ella. It's romantic. Plus, I love their accents."

His boyish grin oozed with charm and Charlene

finally conceded with a blush. "Well, I do like that part."

Cole shot me a quick wink and I had to gulp back my giggles.

The guy was adorable and sexy and cheeky. I could see why girls blushed in his presence; heck, I probably did all the time. The thought brought me up short, and I spent the rest of the meal keeping my eyes away from him and all over my actual boyfriend.

At the end of the meal, we all pitched in our money. David insisted on paying for me, which was really sweet. He was so good like that. Rising from the chair, I gave him a quick kiss.

"Have fun at the game."

"You know I will." His dimple popped into place before he looked over me and said to Cole, "Hey, are you cool to get Ella back to campus?"

"Yeah, of course." Cole didn't look up as he pushed his chair in.

"No, that's okay. I can find my way."

"Baby. Come on. We all know you got lost on the way here." He gave me a smile I knew was meant to be sweet, but it just came across as patronizing.

Not knowing how to respond, I concentrated on lifting my bag onto my shoulder.

"I'll call you after the game, okay?" Kissing my forehead, he moved away from me, getting lost in quick conversation with Mitch.

I turned to Cole, pasting on a cheerful smile. "So, how come you're not going to the game?"

"I declined the invitation."

"Why?" I pulled at a strand of hair the wind was insisting I keep in my mouth.

Cole chuckled. "Soccer's not really my thing."

"Me neither," I moaned. "That's why he didn't bother inviting me, which I really don't mind. It saves me having to say no."

Cole opened his mouth with a slight frown and then shook his head, looking away with a grin. I wanted to ask him what he was thinking, but he started talking before I could. "I'm more of a baseball man."

"You play at school?"

"Yeah, I was a shortstop in the summer and then football was my winter game. I just played for fun, I was never good enough to be taken seriously."

"Plus you have other dreams, right?" I nudged his arm with my shoulder.

"I do." He chuckled and then looked serious as he glanced down at me. "Hey, do you ever ask if they have gluten-free options when you're at a place like that?"

I made a face. "Most of the time it just confuses them, although I think it's getting better. It's becoming more widespread. Restaurants are having to cater. It's just a matter of finding them. The menu's always pretty limited though." I sighed with a smile. "One day, I'd love to walk into a place and know that every single item on that menu was gluten free and I could just order whatever the heck I wanted."

"No more Greek salads for you, huh?"

I snickered. "I guess they're good for me. It'd just be nice to have more options. People like you have no idea how good glutenous food smells. It'd just be nice to eat in a place where I was in the same boat as everybody else."

"Well, if I ever do get my pub up and running, that's what I'm gonna do for you."

I started to laugh.

"I'm serious." He tipped his head at me.

"Cole, you don't have to do that."

"But it'd be cool to try, right?" His hands were in his pockets, his elbows poking out like wings as he shrugged. "I mean, there's bound to be other people on the planet like you. I'm gonna look into it. You can help me write up a gluten-free menu and we'll go for it."

"Sounds good." I nodded with a grin.

Man, it did sound so incredibly good. I would love to help Cole set up his business. His ideas were amazing and it'd be so cool to be a part of it. The fact my insides were buzzing with images of us putting it together enticed me...and then scared me, but I couldn't drop it. The conversation was too much fun, the ideas too alluring to veer away from and for the first time in years, I felt the wings of my heart beating.

We sauntered through Millennium Park, chatting about delicious gluten-free food and how everyday meals could actually be turned gluten-free. We threw menu ideas around and spent that sunny, windy afternoon dreaming without a care.

TWENTY-THREE
ELLA

I forgot reality as I walked home with Cole. It didn't even enter my mind until my feet hit Hyde Park. It was like we'd walked straight into Awkward-ville and our conversation puttered to a stop. Life somehow caught up with me, and I was faced with the truth. No matter how much talking we did, I wouldn't be the one to help Cole build his dreams. That task belonged to another girl; one who wasn't me.

The idea put me in a foul mood, and I spent the rest of the day in my room studying under a rainstorm. David called, all hyper, after the game, asking me to join him for post-match drinks, but I declined, saying I was too tired. I wasn't, but ended up going to bed stupidly early and trying to read. It didn't work, and I spent most of the night in a wallowing stupor.

David was busy studying all day Sunday—what else was new—so I geared up for another lonely day until I noticed Morgan sitting on the couch in her pajamas.

"No Brad today?" I stopped short on my way to the shower.

"Nah." She wouldn't look up from her book.

My eyes narrowed and I snuck around the couch and plopped down next to her.

"What's up?"

"Nothing." She shrugged, flicking the page of her magazine and pulling it close to her face so she could study Anna Kendrick's tan-colored heels. "You know, I think they're being way harsh. She looks hot in that dress and check out those shoes." Morgan pushed the magazine under my nose, but I kept my gaze on her.

"What's up?"

Morgan dropped the magazine with a sigh. "Brad wanted me to sleep over again, and he got all pissy when I declined."

"Why?"

"Because I think he wants to take things up a notch?"

"Why did you decline?"

"Because I feel like we're practically living together, and that's not how I want to spend my senior year."

My eyes narrowed as I studied her. "He's falling in love with you and you're not falling in love with him."

Her sigh was slow and heavy. "We only ever said that this was a college thing. He's from Nebraska, and I don't want to live there. He's got his heart set on moving back home and getting a job near his amazing family, and I...I don't want that."

"So, did you talk about it?"

"Yeah," Morgan flicked the magazine to the floor. "He gets it, but he's annoyed and said maybe we should just break up now rather than stringing things along."

"What do you want to do?"

"I want to keep having fun with him. He's a great guy and he's fun to be around. I guess I don't want to hurt him, which is why I thought it was better to be upfront and honest about how I was feeling."

Man, she was so much braver than me. I seemed to be staying silent for the exact same reasons. Which was worse?

Wanting to be supportive, I squeezed her shoulder. "You did the right thing."

"Then why do I feel like shit?"

I stuck out my bottom lip, mimicking her pout. "We need a hit of Jo-Jo."

Morgan grinned. "Yeah, we really do."

Jumping from the couch, I grabbed my computer and opened the lid. A few seconds later Jody's Skype phone was ringing.

"Hello, you crazy biatch, why are you calling me this early?"

"Because we missed you." Morgan and I squished our smiling faces up to the screen and Jody grinned.

"If I didn't love you so much, I'd hate you right now." She groaned, sitting up and holding her phone up so we could see her clearly. She yawned loudly and then scratched her manic curls. "What are we talking about?"

"Morgan and Brad's failing relationship. Ow!" I rubbed my arm after Morgan's swift punch.

"Would you stop? It's not failing, we just had a little visit to Honest Town last night. It causes friction."

"Morgs, Brad is so into you and the sex is like super-hot, right? He'll come around."

"Yeah, I just feel bad. I don't like hurting him and I can see that I am."

"He's a tough guy, he can take a hit. Besides, it's better that you're open and honest than stringing him along. That'd be crushing."

I swallowed and picked at my nails as the sisters chatted.

"Maybe he's right and we should break up rather than just going along with this farce. I have no intention of marrying him. I guess it's just nice to have someone around."

"Being single is not all bad, you know." Jody's head tipped to the side.

"You're, like, the busiest person on the planet. You don't even have time for a guy anyway."

"I know, but I'm just saying. You shouldn't be afraid to be alone."

"You know I'm not, which is why I'm seriously considering what Brad said. Maybe we should end it."

"But Brad's so nice." I had to interject. I was such a romantic, and breaking up always gave me the willies.

"He is, and like Jody said, the sex is...mmmmm." Morgan licked her upper lip and lightly bit down on her tongue.

I grimaced and slapped her arm. "Gross."

"Oh please, like you can talk, Ella Simmons. You've totally been getting it on with David."

"What are you talking about?"

"Last Saturday morning. A little love-fest in David's room."

"Oooo - tell me more!" Jody leaned toward the camera.

"I don't..." I frowned, feeling my blood run cold.

How the hell did Morgan know about that?

She squeezed my arm. "Why do you think Cole wanted to borrow my noise-canceling headphones?" My mouth went dry while Morgan tittered. "He heard you guys going for it, and he said it was kind of off-putting. I didn't think David got you hot like that."

He didn't.

I slumped back against the couch. "It wasn't him who got me hot."

The girls both gasped in unison, making me freeze. Did I just say that out loud? Kill me now.

I looked at their goldfish expressions and covered my face with my hands.

"Was it Cole?" Morgan asked.

"No!" My head shot up. I glared at Morgan.

"What?"

"We're just friends." My heart was slamming so hard into my chest, I thought it might bounce onto the coffee table.

"Okay." Morgan didn't believe me.

"I—"

"So, who's getting you all steamed up then?" I looked to Jody. Her eyebrow was quirked high, ready for the gossip and I knew I had to spill. With a soft groan, I ran two hands through my hair. "A guy in the shower."

"What?" They both practically screeched the word, and I had to raise my hands just to get them to shut up.

"It's not like that. My first day here, I went and had a shower and started singing, and he joined in from the other side of the wall."

"What were you singing?" Jody's eyes were bright fairy lights.

"A little Ella Fitz and some Louis Armstrong."

"Oh my gosh, and he knew it!"

"Yeah, like perfectly. We sung 'Cheek to Cheek'

and then went straight into 'Can't Take That Away From Me.'"

"No way, he's like your destiny."

"He's not my destiny, Jody. He's just some guy with a really...sexy voice that... that..."

"Gives you fever," Jody sang for me.

I looked at her, my forehead wrinkling. "Yeah."

Morgan's smile was on full beam as she wrapped her arm around my shoulders. "Ella Bella likes a new fella." She giggled. "You have to find him."

"I can't! Come on, you guys, I'm with David! I already feel guilty enough that I was fantasizing about the mystery man while I was having sex with my boyfriend. This is bad! I have to get him out of my head!"

The girls' silence was unnerving. I looked between them.

"I do. I can't pursue this. David is... David's a good guy."

"Yes, he is." Jody nodded.

"But he isn't the only man you ever have to be in love with," Morgan spoke softly.

I clenched my teeth and breathed in through my nose. "He's my boyfriend, Morgan. He's got plans. He wants to get married. It's all mapped out."

"*He's* got plans. *He* wants to get married. Shouldn't you be saying *we* in those sentences?"

I hated Morgan for challenging me on this, but I couldn't look away from her tender expression.

"He's been good to me. He says he'll be lost without me. I make him happy and he deserves my loyalty," I whispered. "I might never find shower guy. Or he might be a horrible person who just happens to have a great singing voice."

"Or he might be the perfect match for you." Jody's eyes were still dancing, her hope making me want to believe her.

"That's not the point, Jody. I might never find him. This campus is huge; there are thousands of people here. I'm not about to start searching for something that is just this implausible, romantic dream."

"But you love romance."

"I am practical enough to know it only exists in movies."

"No you're not. You want it. You've just been settling."

"David is not settling." I pointed at the screen. "He's a good catch."

"We're not denying that, Ella." Morgan rubbed my shoulder. "But is he the best catch for you? That's all we're saying."

I pulled away from her.

"You have to admit that it's kind of creepy to be dreaming about another guy when you're with David," Jody said.

I threw my hands in the air with a huff. "What, so I just break up with him on the off-chance I might meet shower guy?"

"No, you break up with him because he's not right for you anymore."

"He's fine for me. I mean, sure, he doesn't physically affect me like shower guy, but a good relationship should not be based on sex."

"True." Morgan nodded. "It should be based on two people who love each other and want the same things out of life." Her smile faltered. "Which is why I should probably be breaking up with Brad."

My face bunched with sympathy. I squeezed Morgan's shoulder. "You don't have to do that. You love him."

"I do. I really care about him, but we're not heading in the same direction." She shrugged and then looked me square in the face. "Just like you and David."

My eyes filled with tears. I slashed them away as they fell, my voice wobbling. "Morgan, you do what feels right for you, and I'll do what's right for me." I sniffed. "David's a good guy."

"You said that," Jody mumbled.

"His direction is my direction. He can make me...he's a good person." I pointed between them, hating their sad smiles.

"It's okay to be on your own, Ella." Morgan captured my hand in hers.

"It's not...That's not what..."

"Sweetie, you need to stop being so afraid of your own company. Being alone will not kill you."

I licked a tear running past my mouth. "It nearly did, Morgan. I don't ever want to be that fifteen-year-old kid again. You have no idea how terrified I was. You and Jody...and *David* kept me sane. I can't just walk away from that."

"You're a different person now." She squeezed my hands. "You've grown up. You've changed."

"Ella." Jody captured my attention, forcing me to look at the screen. "You don't owe any of us anything, but you do owe it to yourself to figure out what you want and then go after that thing."

I nodded with a weak smile, appreciating her words, but she still didn't get it. She was motivated, driven by the bright lights of Broadway. She'd make it one day too; I could already see her billboard at Times Square. But I wasn't like that. I didn't have the drive and determination of these two women. All I wanted was to never feel as vulnerable as I did waiting in that police station for a social worker to come and collect me.

I wanted safety and David gave me that.

An image of Cole flashed through my mind, and I squeezed my eyes shut.

That could never be an option.

No. David. I had to stick with David. We'd be

happy together. Things would work out fine. Sure, he didn't get my body zinging like shower man, and he didn't make me heart flutter the way Cole seemed to, but that didn't matter. We had something solid and dependable...and besides, leaving him would break his heart, and I couldn't live with that.

TWENTY-FOUR

COLE

"Shit," I mumbled, flicking the spilled beer off my hand and reaching for a towel. Mumbling another apology, I grabbed a fresh glass and pulled a new beer for the customer. He took it with a grin and headed to his table.

Quigg's was busy tonight but not crammed. A solo artist played very mellow tunes on her guitar. Her smoky voice created a nice, soft ambience and the patrons were matching the mood. People often wanted chilled-out music on a Sunday night; with work the next day, they weren't after hype.

I usually liked this tone, but tonight I felt restless and could have used some kick-ass Chaos to get the blood pumping. Yesterday with Ella had been freaking awesome. She was so easy to talk to and she liked my dream. We chatted as if we were planning it together, and I finally got a taste of what Nina and Malachi constantly tried to sell me. I wanted it. I wanted to fall in love and build my dream with someone.

I hated that I'd fallen, but I had. No matter how much I wanted to fight it, I was ready for that next step in my life. It made me feel weak and frustrated...mostly because the girl I wanted to do all this stuff with was unavailable. I couldn't muscle in on my best friend's relationship, although I did have my doubts about whether they were right for each other.

Was I just thinking that because I didn't want them together anymore?

I pictured Ella's face as I asked her about her dreams and shook my head.

No, I was right on some level. I was pretty confident of that.

"Excuse me!"

I glanced down the bar and spotted a sexy brunette trying to get my attention. I pasted on a grin and walked toward her.

"What can I get ya?"

"Just a house wine, please."

"Red or white?"

"Red, of course." Her smile was slow and sensual, and I took a second to admire it. She was pretty damn hot. I glanced back over my shoulder as I stepped toward the wine glasses, wondering if I should have been checking her ID, but she looked older than college. She had a sophistication and confidence to her that made me think she was in her late twenties. Her ample breasts were tucked neatly into a tight purple shirt. It was a tantalizing piece of material that made my traitorous body respond immediately.

Clearing my throat, I reached for a clean glass,

trying to distract myself by thinking of something other than the curve of her milky white breasts, but the only thing my mind could conjure was the curve of another pair of soft breasts that belonged to a songbird. I had imagined what she looked like so many times. She had several different faces and forms. I could never pinpoint which one matched her voice the best. My fears of a limbless, toothless, bald girl had vanished over time, and I had now come to the crazy conclusion that if I ever did meet her, I'd be undone.

Uncorking a fresh bottle of red, I poured it into the glass, making sure I didn't dribble any over the sides. It pissed me off that I would never be undone by shower girl, because she didn't want to meet me. No, she was in love with someone else, and that poor guy didn't deserve my muscling in on that relationship either.

All I wanted was a girl and all I had was nothing.

Placing the glass gently in front of Ms. Brown Eyes, I told her the price and she handed me a twenty, her dark orbs assessing me with a smile.

"I'm Trisha." She held the note out to me.

I grabbed the bill and tried to pull it from her grasp, but she held it steady.

"Cole," I said with a grin.

She let the money go, her teeth brushing her bottom lip. I swallowed, stepping back to the cash register and depositing the cash.

Damn. She would be one hell of a distraction tonight. Maybe I needed it. I hadn't had sex in weeks, and I needed to release a little tension.

Stepping back to her end of the bar, I pressed my hands against the shiny wood and smiled. "So, Trisha, what do you do?"

*****

I caught the slightly-tipsy woman to my side, laughing with her as she stumbled out of Quigg's door. I could feel Nina's eyes burning holes through the back of my head, but I ignored her. I'd done most of the clean-up while Trisha waited on the barstool for me. Nina had tried to kick her out twice, but I'd stood up for the paralegal; I had plans with her tonight.

"Where do you live?" I stopped to hail a cab while she told me her address.

We slipped into the back, and before I'd even gotten the door closed, she was on me. Her lips and tongue explored my face, no doubt getting burned by my evening stubble. She didn't seem to mind; her strong fingers held my head to hers as my hands roamed her body. Damn, she felt good.

We arrived a few minutes later, chucking money at the driver and practically rolling out of the car.

"Over there." She pointed to the apartment block across the road and we headed toward it, an unsettling nervousness brewing in my stomach.

We stopped outside her door and she turned to me, her eyes sparkling. "Do you want to come up?"

I knew what I should have said, but my head bobbed and she tugged me inside. I followed her up the one flight of stairs and nibbled the back of her neck as she unlocked the door, pressing myself against her butt and letting her know my exact intentions.

She didn't seem to mind. The second we were inside, she slammed the door shut and threw herself at me. Pressing her body against me, she moved us back to the couch, her tongue assaulting my neck again. Her breathing was rapid and laced with the smell of wine.

I ran my hands into her hair and tried to focus on the feel of her breasts pushing into my chest and the aching desire in my pants. I needed to relieve this pressure and get my head straight again.

Yanking up my shirt, she pulled it over my head, running her nails lightly down my flesh. My skin prickled.

It felt wrong.

I almost looked away as she whipped off her own shirt and threw it to the floor. Two seconds later, her bra was dangling from her fingertips and I was staring at two very gorgeous breasts.

I reached for them, her eyes lighting with pleasure as I rubbed my thumbs over her nipples.

It felt wrong.

My lips met her neck, and I tried to ignore my thoughts, diving into the erotic moment. I wouldn't stay the night. In an hour or so, I'd be back in my dorm, tucked up in bed with a smile on my face.

My dorm.

Ella.

She'd no doubt be in bed with David.

Ugh. Perhaps I'd go for a shower instead.

Songbird.

"Oh, that feels good." Trisha breathed in my ear as she scrambled for the button of my jeans.

I jerked back.

"What's wrong?" Her eyes rounded as I stepped away from her.

I frowned, running a hand through my hair and clearing my throat.

I couldn't do this.

It felt wrong.

"Why'd you stop?" Trisha put her hands on her hips.

"I don't know you."

"Excuse me?"

"We don't even know each other."

"We just spent the whole night talking." She sniggered.

"Did we?" I reached for my shirt, closing my eyes as I put it on. Tugging it down over my back, I looked her straight in the eye. "You don't know me."

Not like Ella did.

"If you didn't want this, why the hell did you come up?"

"I'm sorry." I stepped away from the couch, grabbing my jacket off the floor. "I thought this would help me forget about my problems, but I...this isn't gonna work for me. I'm sorry."

I tutted, hating that I'd just lost the casual sex card. Stopping at the door, I gave her one more apologetic smile before stepping into the hallway.

"You're such a jerk." I zipped my jacket as I sped down the stairs.

I didn't see a cab anywhere, so I shoved my hands into my pockets and walked to the bus stop. It would take way longer to get back to my dorm, but I needed to cool off.

Hearing Trisha whisper that I felt good just made me feel sick. It was the wrong voice.

Checking that the street was clear, I ran across it and continued my fast-paced clip.

I had wanted Ella's voice in my ear. She knew me. I'd told her stuff that only Nina and Malachi knew...privileged memories and dreams that I kept hidden from everyone. And now the only person I wanted touching me that intimately was her.

I didn't want sex. I wanted to make love...to Ella. Images of her petite body moving in time with mine scorched my brain. I imagined running my hands over her perfect form and looking into her large eyes, having them smile at me, smothering me with sunshine while I slipped inside her. I wanted to make her body tingle, I wanted to send her over the edge of pleasure. I wanted my touch to undo her.

"You're so frickin' screwed, you idiot."

Despair washed over me, my mood becoming blacker with each step. Whether I wanted to or not, I had to get over Ella. This was killing me.

A bus pulled up just as I reached the stop. I jumped on, swiped my card and slumped into a seat near the back, my dark thoughts turning my brain into a maelstrom.

An hour later, I was walking into my room. For a second, I forgot where I was and slammed the door shut. I winced, hoping I hadn't woken David. I glared at his door, wondering if Ella was cuddled up beside him. I didn't want to stick around to find out.

Snatching the towel off the back of my chair, I headed straight out again, closing the door as softly as I could. I needed to wash off Trisha's scent. I needed to unwind. I needed to purge myself of this unrest and get my damn life back.

TWENTY-FIVE
ELLA

I flinched as the door slammed, my head popping off the pillow.

"Damn it, Cole. We're trying to sleep here, you freaking night owl," David mumbled into my shoulder.

Cole.

My body tensed.

I hadn't been able to get him out of my head since my Skype call this afternoon. I'd felt so restless after it finished that I'd left the dorms, needing to walk...to think, to try to work out what the hell I was supposed to do with my life.

The fresh air did me no good. My brain was so filled with scattered thoughts I couldn't control them. Three men whirled before me, and I craved them all for different reasons.

David equaled security.

Cole equaled magic. I felt so alive when I was around him.

And shower guy...shower guy equaled passion. He set my body alight.

So which was the best choice?

My head told me security. It was logical. It made sense. But my heart protested, squeezing inside me and shouting that magic and passion would make my life brilliant.

David had texted me around six, asking me to come over. I went right away, guilt driving me there, along with the desire to try to make our relationship something that it wasn't.

We spent the evening in bed, me trying to get my body fired up, but it just didn't work. Sex with David was nice. It was comfortable, but my body wouldn't sing.

At least David was happy.

He'd moaned and groaned pleasantly throughout both encounters, tucking me against him and feeling triumphant once we were done. I'd laid there tense and silent while he chatted about his day of study. Finally, the light had gone off and we'd drifted to sleep...well, David had.

Reaching for his bedside clock, I looked at the time.

1:05 a.m. There was no way I could lie here awake for the rest of the night. I had classes tomorrow. I needed to be in my own bed.

I shifted the covers and tried to wriggle free of David's embrace.

"Stay," he mumbled.

"I have an early class," I whispered. "And I won't be able to sleep properly if I stay."

"Maybe if you stayed more often, you'd get used to it."

I froze, swallowing down the boulder that was lodged in my windpipe. "I don't think you realize how sexy you are. I'm not gonna be able to sleep with you lying here naked all night."

The lie bolstered his ego, and he relented with a little chuckle, lifting his arm off me. I reached for my clothes and fumbled them on in the dark, not even bothering with my underwear.

"I love you," he muttered sleepily before rolling toward the wall.

"Love you too," I eventually whispered back before sneaking to the door. He was asleep before I even left the room.

I gazed through the dark at Cole's door, wondering if he was sleeping on his bed now. I couldn't help imagining the pleasure of sleeping next to him at night, tucked up against his strong side. I closed my eyes and let out a soft moan.

"It'd be heaven."

I yanked open the door and scurried down the corridor. My room was black and empty, isolation creeping over me as I perched on the edge of my bed. Flicking on the lamp, I squinted in the brightness, taking in my surroundings and feeling that familiar loneliness.

"I need a shower."

A little singing and warmth would ease my mind. I wanted to wash David off me as well, which felt bad. I should have wanted his scent to linger all over my body, but not tonight.

Reaching the bathroom, I eased the door open and headed to the back stall. Flicking on the spray, I undressed quickly and felt the temperature before stepping under the water. I let out a slow sigh.

Yes, this was exactly what I needed.

As always, my thoughts turned to shower guy. I wondered where he was at this exact moment. In bed? Sleeping beside another girl or lying on his own...just waiting for me.

I closed my eyes against the thought and pushed my head under the spray, enjoying the feel of the water washing over me. A song flittered through me, a smile creeping over my lips as it filled me with warmth.

Pulling my head back, I turned to face the shower head and stopped.

A voice filled the space before I could, rounding over the melody of "Let's Call The Whole Thing Off."

It was him.

His smooth voice was punching out a song that always made me smile. Louis Armstrong and Ella Fitzgerald sang the perfect version of it, teasing each other for liking different things, but knowing at the end of the day, in spite of their differences, they couldn't live without each other.

I touched the wall, feeling his words run through me, loving the way they pressed against my skin and filled me with such deep longing. Closing my eyes, I rested my head against the cool tiles and listened.

I wanted to join him. Open my mouth and relish the sound of our voices blending together...but I knew I shouldn't.

He was getting to my favorite part of the song. I loved the way the tune jumped and Ella always nailed it, her sweet voice gifting the song a cheerful beauty.

He sang the line of doubt...questioning what would happen if things were called off, and I responded before I could stop myself, knowing the truth. If things ended now, it would break my heart, just like the song implied.

I heard his shower flick off. The air went still around me. Was he leaving?

Probably. Last time, I'd told him a big fat no and

just walked away when he was still calling out to me.

I deserved nothing less.

Pressing my fingers into the tiles, I tried to ward off the tears, but they didn't have time to fall, because he kept singing. A smile spread across my lips, my insides bursting as he sang the lines, and then I joined him.

There would be no calling off tonight.

He cut the final, long note short and cleared his throat. "Stay there. I'm coming to you."

I flicked off my shower, breaths punching out of me. I knew I should have been calling out and telling him no, but I couldn't. I wanted to see him. I wanted to look into his eyes and know.

I had to put a face to the voice.

Biting my bottom lip, I reached for my towel and wove it around me, not bothering to dry off.

What would happen when we saw each other?

Would he be handsome?

Was he tall, fat, short, skinny? What color was his skin? Did he have brown eyes, blue, green?

Was his hair long?

I bunched my shaking fingers into fists and pulled back the curtain.

The door squeaked open and I held my breath, stepping out of the cubicle.

My insides froze as I caught sight of him, hope sinking through my body and puddling on the floor at my feet.

"Oh, no," I whispered, tears instantly lining my lashes.

TWENTY-SIX

COLE

My mouth dropped open, my eyes transfixed on the exquisite form in front of me.

"Ella." The word came out as a breath. I was too astonished to make another sound.

It couldn't...but it made so much sense.

The pull that I'd felt for her, the way she affected me.

My songbird was the girl I'd been craving.

I smiled. "I can't believe it's you."

She shook her head, a tear escaping.

I stepped toward her, wanting to brush it away. Actually wanting to do a hell of a lot more than that. She stood there in nothing but a towel and my insides were going crazy. Her wet hair, long and straight, caressed the top of her breasts. I wanted to reach out and gather her in my arms, but she raised her hand and moved away from me.

"Don't. It can't be you." She sounded broken, as if this was the worst thing that could have ever happened to her.

It hurt, like a sledgehammer through my chest.

"Why'd you never tell me you could sing?"

"Ditto." She pointed at me.

I grinned and nodded my head, holding the towel around my waist. If it fell, she'd get a glimpse of exactly what I was feeling, and I had a sneaking suspicion that wouldn't fly.

Thankfully she was gazing at my face, staring into my eyes with an agony that was breaking my heart.

"What are we supposed to do now?"

She let out a splintered laugh. "There's nothing we can do. We just have to pretend like this never happened."

"I can't do that."

"He's your roommate. Your best friend. We don't have a choice, Cole." She clutched the towel, her delicate knuckles turning white. "No one can know about this."

I wanted to reason with her, talk sense, but she was right. This was a catch-22 neither of us were prepared for.

Rock, meet hard place.

I closed my eyes with a grimace. "No one will," I finally muttered.

My heart was crushed beneath those words. It didn't help that when I opened my eyes, her face bunched with tears. She was as devastated. That should have been some kind of comfort, but it wasn't.

I couldn't look at her as she grabbed her stuff and fled the room. I was too shell-shocked to follow her. All I knew was that those heartbroken sniffs as she ran away from me would be the only music I'd hear tonight.

TWENTY-SEVEN

ELLA

Professor Mishan's voice washed over me as I sat in class.

My pen whirled over my paper, curving around a large C before circling the o beside it. A second later it was looping up for an l and then swirling around an e.

Cole.

The name stared up at me...a taunting reminder of what I couldn't have.

I scribbled it out and tried to focus back on the professor's words, but I couldn't. All I could see was Cole's half-naked body standing in front of me. I was right; he was Superman.

His chest was broad and perfect, the curve of his muscles turning my legs to jelly. My blood had run hot as I watched him clutch his towel, trying to hold it in place and hide his erection. It hadn't worked.

Man, he'd wanted me. Big time.

If I'd lost control like I'd wanted to, I would have had him there on the cool bathroom floor.

My cheeks grew hot and I rubbed my mouth, squirming in my seat to eradicate the tingles firing between my legs.

It felt like cheating. I know I hadn't done anything, but my mind had made love to Cole in so many ways since that night, and I couldn't seem to make it stop.

It'd been over a week since I'd seen him standing in the girl's bathroom, and the images were still crystal clear. I'd rushed back to my room, thrown myself onto the bed and cried like a baby.

Cole.

Why did it have to be Cole?

It made sense in some ways. We seemed drawn to each other, magic and passion. It was an addictive mix, and I wanted a taste of it so bad. Not just a taste. I wanted to swim in an ocean of it.

The last ten days had been hideous.

I'd been in major avoidance mode, trying to make sure I didn't bump into him. I'd stopped singing in the shower and started spending more and more time with Morgan, who had broken up with Brad and was feeling just as miserable as I was. She said they were going to remain friends, but I had a feeling it was pretty awkward and difficult right now. I think she was appreciating the company.

I hadn't seen Cole in six days. The last time had been uber-uncomfortable. David sat between us at the basketball game, and he would have been completely numb not to feel the tense vibes circling around him. When he'd asked me about it, I'd just said he was imagining things and then blamed my period when I declined his invitation to spend the night.

After lying straight to his face, twice, I'd gone into turtle mode; that was what my dad used to call it.

"Watch out," he'd say, "Ella's in turtle mode again."

It was my way of dealing with things. When something got on top of me, I found it easier to just close off the world, hide inside my shell and keep my lips sealed. I'm sure Mom and Dad used to bet on who could get me to open up first. They had their different prying techniques, and one of them would always break me.

That was now Morgan's job, but like hell I'd let her in on this.

She knew something was up. I knew she'd start working me soon, getting under my skin with her little comments. I remained her grace period for now, but the expiration date loomed near.

Cole had popped around twice this week. The first time, he'd made the mistake of identifying himself. I'd jumped back from the door and crept to my room, hoping he would think I wasn't there. After five minutes he gave up. It was a double-edged sword of disappointment and relief that tore through me as I listened to him walk away.

The second time, Morgan had answered the door, and I hadn't been there. He'd kept his mouth shut about why he wanted to chat to me, and when Morgan asked me about it, I hedged big time, which was why I knew she was getting ready to yank my head out of my shell and make me talk.

She said she wanted a girls' night this weekend, and I had no choice but to agree. I was sort of dreading it, but maybe it would be a relief to get it all off my chest.

My phone vibrated inside my jeans pocket, and I stretched my leg to pull it out. Hiding it under my desk, I read the text and pressed my lips together.

We have to talk about this. You can't keep ignoring me. Please. Just one conversation.

I squeezed the phone in my hand, knowing Cole was right. He'd been texting me daily, and I'd quickly deleted each one.

I couldn't see him.

Not because I didn't want to. We did need to talk this out some more, try to find some even ground we could walk on. David's suspicions would grow if he could never get the two of us together again.

I was just afraid that if I was alone with Cole for even a minute, I'd lose all self-control.

David deserved my loyalty.

I couldn't break his heart and run off with his best friend. That was all kinds of wrong.

I wouldn't be that girl.

No, there was nothing we could do. I just had to stay away from Cole until I was over him...then David and I could get on with his plans for our future.

Damn it, that sounded so wrong. Why was I staying with David? I knew in my heart I should have been rehearsing my break-up speech, but every time I imagined it, my insides turned to ice. I couldn't look David in the eye and finish a three-year relationship; the very idea was petrifying. I loved him. Yes, Cole did things to me, but did that give me the right to break David's heart? I couldn't hurt him. I couldn't do it.

Swiping my thumb over the screen, I pressed the red delete box and Cole's message disappeared.

TWENTY-EIGHT

COLE

I muttered a curse and dumped my phone onto the bar.

She still hadn't replied. I'd been checking my phone all damn day and nothing.

How could she be so stubborn?

We had to talk this through, even if the outcome wasn't what we wanted. Now that I was over my shock, I was levelheaded enough to recognize that we needed to exchange serious words.

It wasn't like I was going to ask her to dump David and move in with me. Although I'd love that, I'm not a heartless bastard.

I just missed her, and getting back to being friends was better than nothing. I wasn't dumb enough to think that things could ever be the same.

There would forever be a slight discomfort between us now. I wanted her. Bad. I couldn't help wondering if she wanted me too, but I knew she was loyal and David would win this one. She certainly wouldn't break up with him to be with me. No, if she ever did decide to leave him, it had to be for her.

My phone dinged, and I nearly tripped over myself getting back to the bar.

Malachi chuckled at me as he sat down the other end, going over some paperwork.

I hurried to unlock my phone and my shoulders slumped as I read the text.

"Not the one you were hoping for, eh boy?"

"Nah," I sighed. "It was just Quinn letting me know about that swing band. They're playing at a club on Saturday night. I'll pop down and see if they're a good fit for here."

"A swing band? In this place?"

"I've heard really good things about them. Maybe they can do a mellow jazz set."

"Oooo, that sounds divine." Nina closed the door to their apartment and shimmied across the empty floor. "I can just picture it. A few Louis vibes floating through the room. Do they have a female singer?"

"Not sure." I shrugged. "I guess I'll find out this weekend."

Nina headed to the stereo system, picking up the iPod and scanning for a playlist. Moments later, Ella Fitzgerald started singing "Summertime," and I wanted to curl into a ball and die. I could imagine my Ella nailing this song.

"Not *your* Ella, you asshole," I muttered.

"What did you just say?" Nina's green eyes rounded.

"Nothing."

Her red hair spilled over her shoulder as she

tipped her head to the side and looked at me. Approaching me cautiously, she held out her hand. "Dance with me."

"Not today, Nina." I pressed my back against the bar.

"Cole Reynolds, when a lady that beautiful asks you to dance, you don't say no." Malachi dropped his pen and glared at me.

With a sigh, I took Nina's hand and let her guide me to the dance floor. Taking her into my arms, the way she showed me how, I took the lead and we began a slow shuffle across the wooden floor.

"Tell me your woes."

"I really don't want to talk about it."

"That may be the case, but you need to. So spill."

I squeezed her hand and pushed her away for a slow spin before bringing her back to my side.

"I'm falling in love with a girl I can't have."

Nina's lips twitched. I could tell she was reining in a full-blown smile.

"It hurts, Nina."

Her green gaze filled with affection. "Why can't you have her?"

"Because she's with David."

"Are you talking about that gorgeous little thing that was here a few weeks ago? She stayed to help us clean up."

"That's the one."

"I liked her." Nina's freckled cheeks rose with a smile.

"There's no point in you doing that." I dipped Nina then pulled her back up and spun her away from me. "She's pretty loyal to the guy."

"Do you think they're suited?"

"No. He doesn't see her. I don't even think he knows that she can sing like an angel. She's with him, but it's like she's afraid to give him everything. I don't—I don't know if I'm just saying that because I want her with me."

"But she's opened up to you."

"Sometimes I wonder if I know her better than he does...and they've been together for three years now."

"So why does she stay with him?"

"Beats me!" I huffed.

"Do you think she likes you, too?"

I paused, looking down at Nina, my smile broken. "I thought I felt a connection, but maybe I was wrong."

"You're not. I saw it, when she was here that night."

"She's not mine, Nina." My voice broke. "And now I don't want anything else." I dropped her arms and paced away from her. "That woman I left with the other night, I couldn't go through with it. I don't want casual sex anymore, and thanks to you guys and your crap about being a team and building your dreams together, that's all I want! You guys totally screwed me over!"

Nina looked at Malachi, who gazed back at her before letting out a loud guffaw. "Oh, you've really got it bad, Boy-o."

"Shut up, Malachi. This frickin' sucks."

"Mac the Knife" started to play, and I grabbed Nina up again. I'd take this upbeat tune over the melancholy crap any day. Nina wouldn't take her eyes off me as I held my head high and tried to avoid her gaze. As the song drew to an end, I dipped her and she caught my gaze.

"Life has a way of working out, Cole. God's not into torturing people."

"Do you always have to bring your faith into every conversation?" I drew her north with a hard snap before letting her go.

"It's part of who I am, so yes. I do." She put her

hands on her hips. "I'm not asking you to believe in him, I'm just telling you what I think."

"Well, you're wrong about the torture thing, because he's put me through plenty."

She sighed, her expression growing even more tender. "I know you haven't had the easiest life, but good things have come for you too."

"How is this good?" My voice wobbled, tears burning at my eyes. I pressed my thumb and forefinger into my sockets, forcing the feeling away.

Nina's hands landed on my arms, gently rubbing my taut biceps.

"You know when you first came to us and you were this hurting, lost kid?"

I glanced at her.

"I fell in love with you instantly, Cole. I saw something so precious in your gaze. It helped me hold tight when you had those tantrums and that time you tried to run away." She chuckled. "Do you remember what I used to say to you once you'd calmed down?"

I looked to the floor, squeezing the back of my neck. "You said that sometimes we have to wade through the muck to reach higher ground. You promised me that I would find my way."

"And you did."

I snickered, resting my hands on my hips and clenching my jaw. "I don't feel like it right now."

"Honey, you know I would never wish any kind of heartache on you, but you have to believe that something good is going to come out of this. You'll eventually reach your higher ground, and you'll be stronger and wiser than you were before. There's always a bigger picture in play. You have to cling to that hope."

"Yeah, yeah, I know." I flicked my hand dismissively and then shot her an apologetic smile.

With a slow nod, I let out a sigh. "She feels so right for me, Nina. She's my one and I can't have her."

"You can't see into the future. Who knows what a little patience will achieve."

"Good things come to those who wait, right?" I rolled my eyes.

"Well, and to those who fight for it." She grinned. "She's obviously not ready for you to do that yet. You just need to bide your time. Accept where she's at."

"But what if she just lets David keep controlling her future? What if she doesn't figure it out?"

"Cole, you have to trust that if she's meant to be yours, she will be...and if there's someone better for you out there, then your feelings for Ella will fade."

I couldn't imagine it, not for a heartbeat. The second I worked out that she and Songbird were one and the same, I knew...right down to my very core. Ella was the girl for me.

TWENTY-NINE

ELLA

Morgan still hadn't said anything. It made me nervous. It was Saturday night and we were supposed to be hitting the town, just me and her. That was what she'd said anyway. She was being way too mysterious for my liking. I expected pajamas, ice cream, and some serious conversation, but she pulled out my dark purple dress that was more like a sleeve with straps and told me to fancy up.

"I'll be back in an hour, and we can finish getting ready together."

She slipped out before I could ask where she was going.

I now stood in front of my mirror in nothing but my black panties and bra, carefully applying eyeliner.

The front door jiggled and I dropped the stick, smearing black ink down my hand. Glancing out into the living area, I was about to demand Morgan tell me where I was going when my voice evaporated.

Dumping the eyeliner on my desk, I raced into the living room with a squeal.

"Jody!"

We wrapped each other in a tight embrace, laughing and jumping around in a circle.

"What are you doing here?" I held her at arm's length, drinking in her sunny smile and bright green eyes.

"Morgan called an SOS. She said you guys needed some sunshine...and sunshine is here." She pointed at herself and wiggled her eyebrows.

I burst into laughter and pulled her into another embrace.

"Now, I can only stay for one night, so we have to make it count."

"Where are we going?"

Morgan dumped Jody's bag next to the couch and grinned at me. "You're gonna love it."

"Hells yeah!" Jody lifted her arms into the air and swayed her body.

"Dancing? We're going dancing?"

"Not just any kind of dancing." Morgan beamed. "Brad's a bouncer tonight at this club in town. They've got this amazing band playing, and he's already promised me he'll get us in."

"Are you and Brad back together?"

Morgan blushed, wrinkled her nose and then tipped her head to the side. "Maybe?"

"Morgan."

"No, I know, I know, it's just...I've missed him so much more than I thought I would, and I just want to give it one more try. I don't want to walk away from something that is maybe right for me, and Brad finally suggested he might be willing to consider living somewhere other than his home town after graduation, so..." She gave a little gleeful smile.

I grinned back, feeling happy for her. They did seem good together. There was definite chemistry between them. My smile faltered, my own woes crashing back over me.

Morgan's face crumpled with concern. "But this night is not about boys. It's about the Terrible Trio going out to have a little fun."

"It's time to shake our asses," Jody sang, making us all giggle.

"Let's suit up." Morgan clapped her hands and I rushed back into my room.

Eyeing the purple dress on my bed, I wrinkled my nose and turned back to my closet. Flicking through the hangers, my hand landed on the dark red dress I'd bought on a whim last year. The fabric was silky soft and draped my body perfectly, but the main reason I'd fallen in love with it was the knee-length skirt. It was a twirly dress, and I had only worn it once since Jody made me try it on. We'd gone out that night and twirled on the beach, looking ridiculous, but feeling freer than birds as our skirts spun wide in the night air.

Stepping into the snazzy number, I called Jody to help zip me up. The dress sat really low on my spine, exposing my back.

"Take your bra off." Jody tittered. "The strap runs right across your back. It looks awful."

I did as commanded and wriggled out of it, throwing it on my bed before doing a slow spin and then clutching my breasts.

"How am I going to dance without a bra?"

"You're not that big." Jody's eyes rounded. "No offense."

MELISSA PEARL

I poked my tongue at her and she giggled. "Well, do a few moves, see how it feels."

I jiggled around, feeling like a fool and soon crumpling into fits of giggles on the floor. Jody pulled me back up, her own limbs weak from laughter.

"I think you'll be fine." She brushed the tears from her eyes. "Do you remember that night at the beach?"

"Yeah," I giggled. "I haven't worn it since." I bit my lip. "I don't think I've laughed this hard since then, either."

"Ah! You look so hot!" Jody stepped back from me and clapped her hands before reaching into the closet and pulling out my strappy sandals.

"There's no way I can dance in those."

"Come on. They suit the dress perfectly."

"Jody." I grabbed her shoulders. "I need to dance tonight."

"You need to dance?"

"I *need* to dance."

Her expression softened as she took in my serious gaze. Her hands touched my elbows. "What's going on?"

"Please, don't make me talk about it right now. I have to switch off."

"We just hate seeing you being eaten up like this. You have to tell us what's wrong." Morgan's head popped up behind Jody's.

"Turtle Mode for two weeks is way over the limit. You better fess up in the morning or I'm gonna have to give that butt of yours a spanking." Jody pointed her finger at me.

I snickered and shook my head, not missing the worried glance Jody threw over her shoulder.

"I guess we'll just have to get you drunk then." She shrugged, making me giggle as Morgan's head began to shake.

"You know what, Morgan, getting drunk sounds brilliant right now." I tipped my head.

She rolled her eyes and gave me a pointed look. "All right, maybe one drink, but no more. We're going there to dance, not get wasted."

"That's right." Jody mocked Morgan's motherly tone. We both laughed while Morgan huffed off to finish getting ready.

Jody dropped the sandals back into my closet and pulled out my white pumps with the gold edging. "Stylish, yet comfortable."

"Perfect."

As soon as we were dolled up, we snapped a quick selfie and headed out the door. Heads turned as we giggled our way down the corridor, but I barely noticed. I was with my girls, and tonight I wanted to forget that men even existed.

The club was humming when we arrived. Brad waved us straight through, giving us all appreciative smiles. Morgan planted a grateful kiss on his lips and promised him a proper thank you later. I looked away from their hungry gazes and made a face at Jody. She licked her upper lip and did a sexy little shimmy, giving me the giggles.

Man, I didn't need alcohol when I was around Jody. She made me drunk on laughter alone. We pressed our way through the crowds and found ourselves a table that looked out over the dance floor. It was a prime spot that had just been vacated. We dumped our stuff and hit the dance floor immediately.

The band was amazing. The lead guy sounded like Michael Bublé, and I nearly died when I saw the brass section rise up behind him.

"Swing!" I screamed at Morgan, grinning like a kid in a candy store. "I love you!"

"I knew you would!" She grabbed my hand and spun me around as the three of us laughed our way through some old jazz routines we'd worked out one summer break. They'd wanted to know the moves my parents had taught me, and as much as I hadn't wanted to do it, it'd been a really cleansing experience.

After dancing hard out to four songs, we fell against each other breathless.

"I'm gonna order some drinks!" Morgan yelled at us.

"Shots!" Jody clasped her hand. "Please!"

"Jody, no!"

"Oh come on." I pulled at her other hand. "Just one."

We put on our pleading faces, and it didn't take much for her to chuckle. "All right, fine! But just one!"

She pushed her way to the bar, and Jody and I decided to dance one more number before heading over to the table. Morgan met us for the end of the song.

"The drinks are on their way."

"Sweet!" Jody started heading for our table.

"I just want to grab a bottle of water first," I called to the girls, moving toward the bar.

My heart was thumping in time with the rhythm; it was a heady rush. I felt elated and free, just what I needed. Finally making it to the bar, I leaned against the metal and attempted to catch the bartender's eye.

"Nice dress!" I spun at the sound of the rich voice behind me and came in contact with a gorgeous pair of blue eyes. His smile was appreciative and melted my heart.

"Hey, Cole." I turned away from him, my giddy high evaporating. He looked way too sexy standing there in his black slacks and white shirt; the dressy-casual style suited him. He looked like a movie star out for a night of fun, ready to dance and turn girls' hearts to marshmallow.

"You look really beautiful tonight."

I pressed my lips together, wishing he wouldn't say stuff like that to me.

"What are you doing here?" I snapped around to face him, my tone sharper than I meant.

He gave me a soft smile, his eyes tender and sweet. "Well, as you know, I really like this kind of music."

My lips stretched into a smile before I could stop them. I glanced down to the bar top and tucked a curl behind my ear.

With a huff, he stepped into my space. "I can't keep doing this, you know."

I looked up, meeting his steady gaze and feeling myself weaken.

"Not talking about it? It's not working for me."

"Cole, I can't—" I tried to back off, but he took my arm, gently holding me.

"Look, just let me say my piece, and then I won't ever mention it again, I promise."

His gaze was so sincere, I had to say yes. "Okay."

I relaxed in his grasp, and he let my arm go. Leaning against the counter, he gave me a sad smile. "We both know it's complicated, and I...uh...know that I'm not gonna get what I want out of this equation. I've accepted that. You're with David, and I respect that one hundred percent, but I just..." He tutted and shook his head, turning to me with an earnest look that made my spine tingle. "I want you to be happy."

"I am." I couldn't look him in the eye. "David's good for me."

"Is he?"

"Don't do this, Cole." I tried to back away, panic sizzling through me. He snatched my wrist, softening the move by rubbing his thumb gently over my skin.

"I'm sorry. You're right. It's not my place." The sad torture cresting over his expression made me want to cry. He had the world's kindest eyes. Why the hell did he have to be so amazing?

He let out a shaky sigh, and a small grin touched his mouth as if he was reminding himself of something. "I know you love him, and you don't want to hurt him. Ella, you're a really good person, and he's lucky to have you." The fact he was giving in stung, but it was such a huge relief. I didn't want a fight, not with Cole. In spite of that, I couldn't help my deflation as he gave me a stiff nod and let me go, shoving his hand into his pocket. I thought he was about to give me a curt goodbye and walk away, but he pressed his lips together and forced a smile. "Look, can we just maybe...be friends, at least?"

My neck muscles were straining as I tried to shake a no. That was what I was supposed to do, right?

Cole leaned into my space again. "David knows something's up with you. Don't think he hasn't noticed. If you don't stop acting so weird around me, he's gonna start making his own conclusions. Incorrect ones."

I swallowed and ran my fingers down my drop earring.

"So for David's sake, can you please just be my friend?" He followed up his emphatic look by sticking out his hand, asking me to accept what he was offering.

I knew I should have walked away, but I didn't want to. I wasn't some dumb, immature kid who couldn't control herself. I could do this. Cole was right. I couldn't have David thinking the wrong thing.

With a tight smile, I clasped Cole's hand and

gave it a little squeeze.

"Thank you." He really meant it.

My smile grew to full beam. It felt good and not as hard as I thought it might have been.

Cole turned his back to the bar and leaned against it. I joined him, deciding to wait for the bartender to head this way before catching his attention.

Without knowing it, my foot started tapping, and I noticed Cole grin at me.

"'Steppin' Out.' It's one of my favorites too."

I chuckled. "How can it not be? It's such a great song," I yelled to him as the music grew louder.

He leaned toward me, making my skin ignite. I tried to ignore the feeling and just listen to his words.

"Can you dance?"

I glanced up at his face and shrugged. "Can't most people, to some degree?"

"No, no." He shook his head with a grin. "I mean, can you really dance?" His eyebrows rose. "Like Fred and Ginger dance."

My lips twitched as I tried to hold back my grin. "Maybe." I peered at him sideways.

His laugh was deep and rich as he grabbed my hand. "Come on, my little friend, you gotta show me."

With a laugh, I let him pull me onto the floor.

I glanced over at Morgan and Jody, giving them a little wave as I started to jive around the floor with Cole. Morgan's eyebrow arched high in question, and I looked away just as Jody leaned toward her with wide eyes and pointed at us. Yep, my little sis was about to find out all about Cole.

I glanced across at my handsome partner. Man, he could really move. Pulling on my hands, he swung me around, taking the lead with confidence. He knew what he was doing, and it brought back memories of dancing in the living room with my dad. The giddy high returned and my cheeks started hurting from smiling so hard. When he threw me up over his shoulder and let me flip to my feet, I thought my heart might fly right out of my chest. I was dipped, twirled, lifted, and spun until I was out of breath with laughter.

We finished the song, both chuckling together and clapping our hands for the band.

I wanted to stay in the moment forever. I was having so much fun. I could tell Cole was, too. His eyes were like Christmas lights.

"Who taught you how to dance?" I asked.

"Nina. You?"

"My dad." My shoulder hitched up in a half-shrug.

"You're really good, you know. Why the hell are you studying literature? You should be dancing."

"I could say the same thing to you. Business studies?" I made a face.

He laughed. "It's all for a reason, Ella. I enjoy dancing, but I've got bigger dreams."

I did know. Dreams I wanted to be a part of.

I swallowed back the thought and nodded, my smile evaporating.

"Well, I guess I should get back to my friends." I pointed over my shoulder and turned to leave, but he grabbed my fingers and tugged me to a stop.

His expression was like melted chocolate as he held up his finger. "Just one more?"

I bit the corner of my mouth and looked over my shoulder at the girls then back at Cole. I couldn't resist his sweet gaze, so I stepped back into his space. "Just one."

His smile grew as he pulled me into his arms and a woman stepped up to the microphone. Her husky voice oozed through the sound system and my heart hitched as she began Peggy Lee's "Fever."

Cole's eyes locked with mine, and I couldn't have looked away if I'd wanted to.

His strong arms held me tight, guiding me around the floor, and everyone else in the club disappeared. It was just me, him, and a sultry voice singing about every feeling Cole sparked inside of me.

I spun around Cole, being drawn back to his body and relishing the fire sizzling through my veins. I couldn't take my eyes from his. We were locked together in a moment that was out of our control.

He dipped me, his hand skimming up my thigh and pulling my knee to rest against his hip. As he pulled me straight, he kept his fingers tucked beneath my knee, holding me to him, and I couldn't resist.

My hand snaked around his neck and I reached for him. He met me halfway, our lips sparking together, igniting a fire that swept through my body. My fingers wove into his curls as his hand spread over my bare back and then moved up to my shoulders. His hot tongue skimmed my lips and I opened my mouth to him, his taste turning my insides to molten lava.

I wanted him. I wanted all of him right now.

My eyes snapped open as if coming out of a daze.

I jerked away, touching my lips with shaking fingers before wriggling out of his grasp. We both stared at each other, bug-eyed, wondering what the hell just happened.

"I'm sorry." I stumbled back, nearly tripping. Righting myself, I turned away from him as the song came to a sizzling end. I made it to my table out of breath.

The girls both stared at me, mouths open, eyes wide.

"So, that was freaking hot," Jody finally said.

I grabbed the shot glass sitting in the middle of the table and looked at them. "Cole's the shower guy." I threw back the shot and slammed it onto the table. The alcohol seared my insides, burning a trail through my system as I took in their shell-shocked expressions. Grabbing my bag, I sniffed at my tears and fled toward the exit.

THIRTY

COLE

I watched Ella down her shot, wince, and then run for the exit. It hurt to watch her, mostly because all I could do was stand there, paralyzed on the dance floor.

I swear when I'd asked her to dance, I had no intention of kissing her, but having her body move beneath my hands had sent me to another kind of heaven...one where I had no control. She felt exquisite beneath my fingers, and the way her eyes locked with mine was hypnotic. When she moved her lips to mine, I was pulled by a force greater than myself.

My stomach coiled as I relived the kiss. My tongue still burned, aching for more.

Someone accidentally bumped me from behind

as the song "Anything Goes" came to a finish. She was very apologetic. I forgave her with a tight smile and left the floor, making my way swiftly out the exit. I couldn't stay here now. I was glad I'd come to hear the band, and I would text the two lead singers to see if they wanted to do a light acoustic set at Quigg's. I could picture it all perfectly, the stage set-up and the song list I'd request. Nina would love it.

So would Ella.

My hand bunched into a fist, and I resisted the urge to punch the door before swinging it open.

"Hey, man. Leaving so soon?" Brad's white smile was blinding.

"Yeah, I...uh..."

"I just saw the girls shoot out of here. Something go on inside?"

My lower lip popped out as I shrugged my shoulders. "No idea."

Brad chuckled. "Girls, right?"

"Yep." My laughter was hard and forced. I slapped Brad on the shoulder and quickly moved past him, knowing I couldn't hold it together for much longer.

I couldn't help scanning the street for three fleeing women, but I didn't see them anywhere. I wondered who the young blonde had been with them. My guess was Morgan's little sister; they looked similar.

Kicking the curb with the toe of my shoe, I decided to head back to the dorm. I guessed Ella wouldn't run into David's arms tonight. She'd been pretty edgy around him lately...probably only in the times I was around. I knew David thought something was off, but he seemed pretty absorbed in his studies so wasn't really taking the time to figure out why. He was also excited about his twenty-first birthday. The party was next weekend, and I knew Ella couldn't avoid me then.

We had to figure out a way to make this work.

Running my hands through my hair, I gulped back a groan.

If she wasn't so damn intoxicating, I could do this.

Maybe I should keep encouraging her to break up with David, but not just because of me. In my opinion, they weren't right together, and she obviously wanted me as much as I did her. But what right did I have to say that to her? How could I, in good conscience, encourage her to break my friend's heart?

David was a good guy. A little obsessive, a little controlling, but his heart was in the right place.

I crossed the road, jumping into a run as a car came around the corner. I hopped back up onto the curb and kept heading for the dorm.

There was no way I could sit down and tell David how I felt. The guy would feel completely betrayed. No, I just had to sit this one out and let Ella make the next move. Damn, that was gonna be hard; watching from the sidelines was not my style.

In spite of how bad I felt about the kiss, I couldn't keep a smile from cresting over my lips as time gave my emotions a chance to settle. She'd kissed me. She'd wanted me. I had felt her hunger, and it was a comfort to know the feelings were mutual.

Surely she was sitting with her girls right now, talking through this dilemma.

I knew I couldn't make up Ella's mind for her, but maybe our little tryst on the dance floor had been exactly what we needed. She'd be lying if she told me I didn't affect her.

Hyde Park was upon me, and I felt a touch lighter as I walked through the darkness and reached my dorm. I knew there was a mire of shit to wade through before I reached this higher ground Nina talked about, but for the first time since meeting Ella, I could almost picture her on the other side, waiting for me. We could do this. It wouldn't be without its heartache, and I didn't know how we'd get around the David factor, but if we were patient, wounds would heal and maybe we could be together.

The idea was so thrilling that a grin broke out on my face as I pushed my dorm room door open.

David sprung from the couch the second I stepped in. At first I couldn't read his expression, and I was worried that maybe Ella had swung by and confessed all, but there was a skittish excitement lurking in his eyes that made me rule out that scenario.

"What's up, man?" I shoved my hands in my pockets, trying to read him.

David grinned, his dimple popping into place as he gave a shaky nod. "I'm gonna do it."

"Do what?"

Sucking in a quick breath, David leapt around the couch and lifted a small box out from between the cushions. My heart plummeted through my body as he came toward me, gently popping the lid. Inside was a ring with a sparkling diamond perched on top.

"I'm gonna ask Ella to marry me."

My tongue felt like sandpaper and stuck to the roof of my mouth when I tried to speak. My eyebrows rose and I blinked twice.

"I know I was gonna wait until after I graduated, but Ella's been really edgy the last couple of weeks, and I just want her to know that in spite of all my study and the fact I'm not seeing her as much as I thought I would, I'm still really committed to her."

"Are you—" I scratched the edge of my mouth.

"Are you sure that's why she's edgy?"

"Come on. It's Ella." He made a face. "She needs security. Ever since getting here, she hasn't been quite as relaxed, and I think she's worried that maybe things are changing between us. I want her to know that the plan is still in place."

The fucking plan. I hated that damn thing.

I pressed my lips together and managed a small smile. "You guys are still pretty young, you know. Are you sure you're not rushing into this?"

"I know what I want, Cole. Rearranging the timeline a little won't make a difference. It's not like we'll be walking down the aisle this summer or anything, but I like the idea of being engaged to her. We can get married next summer, after I graduate." He snapped the box closed. "Mom will insist we get married in L.A. We'll probably go for a reception at the club or something. I'll have to invite Ella's whacked-out aunt." He made a face before rushing on. "And I know she'll choose Jody and Morgan for bridesmaids."

I nodded, keeping my mouth closed against the bile rising up my throat.

"And, of course, I'll be asking you to be my best man." His smile was so broad, he looked like a giddy school kid, and it turned my heart to charcoal.

I punched out a laugh that felt more like a sob and nodded. "Of course, man."

He opened the box again, admiring the diamond inside. "So, I'm gonna ask her at my birthday party."

My mouth fell open. "In front of everyone? Do you think Ella will like that?"

I knew she wouldn't. She'd hate it. Even if she planned on saying yes, she wouldn't like the pressure of everyone around her. Hell, I'd be there.

What would she say?

This was going to shock the shit out of her.

"Don't you think it'd be better to wait for a more intimate moment? You asking will be a massive surprise for her."

"She'll get a kick out of it. It'll be great. All our friends will be there. We can celebrate right away." He closed the box. "I know it's supposed to be my night and everything, but I don't mind sharing the limelight for this."

My eyes stung as he let out a giddy chuckle.

"You gotta swear you won't tell her though, okay? Don't tell anyone. I want it to be a really big surprise. Promise me, man."

I had no good reason not to promise him.

Well, I did. I had one freaking gigantic reason, but David didn't need to hear that.

Maybe it would have been better to just tell him right then, but I didn't say a word. I just gave him a big smile and nodded.

There was no guarantee on this planet that Ella wouldn't say yes. It wasn't my right or my place to tell him about our connection in the shower or the kiss on the dance floor. That was Ella's job, and my biggest fear now was that she wouldn't have the guts to do it.

"Only one week to go!" David spun around and vaulted back over the couch.

Yeah. One week.

Damn, it was going to be a week from hell.

THIRTY-ONE

ELLA

I pressed my lips together and wiped the edge of my mouth, making sure my pink lipstick was as neat and perfect as possible. I didn't usually wear this color, but it matched the dress David bought me for my nineteenth birthday, and I knew he'd want me to wear it tonight. He had been buzzing all week about his big birthday party. I knew his twenty-first was a big deal, but it was also just a birthday. I had no intentions of having a big birthday party for mine. Ultimately, I'd love to just go out with my girls and dance my ass off.

A smile twitched my lips as I remembered jumping around the floor with Morgan, losing myself to Chaos's intoxicating beat. My mind inevitably jumped to a different dance floor and a very different beat. That memory was never far from my mind. I didn't think I'd ever be able to listen to Peggy Lee's "Fever" again. My fingers shook as I slipped my lipstick into my makeup bag and zipped it closed.

I hadn't seen Cole since last Saturday. He hadn't tried to text me, and I knew that shouldn't have bothered me, but it did. We had this huge thing hanging between us and I felt like there was nothing I could do to fix it. Well, I could break up with David, but would that fix it? The fact Cole hadn't made one attempt to connect after that dynamite kiss was unnerving. Maybe he didn't want me after all, and if that was the case, I might as well stay with David. Disappointment seared through me and I hated myself for it. David was a good catch! What the hell was wrong with me?

Besides, I couldn't forget the friendship between Cole and David. It made everything a million times more complicated.

I swallowed and blinked rapidly, not wanting to ruin my eye makeup.

It was better this way. Cole and I obviously couldn't just be friends, so we had to be nothing...except when we were around David, and then we had to pretend that everything was okay.

I closed my eyes and leaned against my desk.

"This is such shit." I sucked in a breath that was a borderline sob and stood straight. Sniffing back my angst, I straightened my back and gazed in the mirror. "You can do this."

Tonight was going to suck. Even if Cole and I stood on opposite sides of the room, it'd be impossible not to look at him. It would be awkward and exhausting. Dread didn't even begin to describe it.

Wiggling my hips, I pulled the tight coral fabric a little further down. I hated its tendency to ride up my thighs. I knew David would love it though. It'd make him happy, which in turn made me happy...or it used to.

I frowned.

Thank God his parents weren't there tonight. His brother Luke was flying in from New York, but the rest of the family was planning on having a party for David over the Christmas break. Another event to look forward to. I rolled my eyes. I so wasn't into this swanky to-do. David kept on describing the hotel as classy, which meant it was like a ten-star for me. The food would be catered and amazing. I, no doubt, could eat none of it, but that didn't matter. David was happy, which in turn made me happy.

I frowned again. Tears scorched my eyes. I snatched a Kleenex out of the box and pressed it into my eyes. There was no way my mascara was going to survive the night if I didn't pull my shit together.

Once I'd pressed the tears into submission, I dabbed beneath my eyes and made sure I was blotch-free. Shaking my fingers, I breathed out. "You can do this, Ella. Just smile and nod."

I slipped my feet into my high, strappy heels and snatched my clutch purse off the bed. Gripping it with tight fingers, I walked into the living room. Morgan slid her phone into her own purse and glanced over at me. She looked stunning in her midnight-blue dress, her blonde hair swept up in a loose bun. Her silver drop earrings came to just above her shoulders.

"Wow, you look great."

She grinned at me, appreciating the compliment.

I did a dip, forcing a cheesy smile. "How do I look?"

"Miserable." Her head tipped to the side with a sad smile, and I felt my insides splinter.

"Morgan, stop!"

"I can't. I know you don't want to talk about it, but you're like my sister and I can't keep watching you do this."

I didn't want to relive my Sunday morning cry-fest with the girls. It had drained me completely and we'd gotten nowhere. I clenched my jaw. "I'm not breaking up with David so that I can be with Cole. It's wrong!"

Morgan shook her head. "You didn't see you and Cole on that dance floor. It was magic, Ella. It's like you guys were dancing in this bubble, like the world around you didn't even exist. You guys have a connection."

"I'm not denying that, but he's David's *best* friend. It doesn't matter whether I want him or not. I can't have him!" I threw my arms wide.

Morgan's head jerked to the side and she clicked her tongue, a sure sign she disagreed with me. "Okay, fine." She nodded, tapping her finger against her purse. "Let's take Cole out of the equation then. Let's pretend he doesn't even exist." Her dark gaze bored into me. "Now picture next year or three years from now or ten years from now...where do you want to be?"

My throat began to swell. I opened my mouth to speak, but nothing came out.

Morgan stepped toward me, bending down so she could get right in my face. "Ella, if David's not in those images in your head right now, then it's not fair for you to keep stringing him along. You're part of his plan. You know he has no intention of breaking up with you."

"Which is why I can't hurt him."

"Sweetie." Morgan grabbed my shoulders. "Do you think it will hurt less now, or when you're walking out the door with his two-point-four children?"

"I would never divorce him."

"So, you'll die an unhappy woman then?"

"Morgan, stop it!" I flicked her hands off me and stepped away from her, my ankle turning in the high heels. I grabbed the couch and winced.

"Ella, you need to figure out what you want...for *you*. I don't think David is it anymore, and if you don't put a stop to it now, it's just gonna get harder."

"I know that! But I can't dump him on his birthday." I threw the excuse into the air and felt instantly guilty. This was the first time I'd admitted to even wanting to break up with him. Well, the first time I'd said it aloud anyway. Somehow that made it more concrete.

It hurt. Three years. David was the only guy I'd ever been with. I thought he'd be my always and forever. I hated that things were changing. I just didn't think I had it in me to break his heart.

In contrast to my inner hurricane, Morgan stood there calmly smiling. "I'd never ask you to dump him on his birthday. I'm just asking you to think about your future and figure out if you want what David has planned. They're his dreams...but are they yours?"

"I don't know what my dreams are and he loves me and he's been loyal."

"Yes, he has, but that doesn't mean you owe him eternity."

I blinked at my stinging tears, my lips bunching together, trying to contain the cry of agony I wanted to unleash. I sucked in two sharp breaths and whispered, "It'll break his heart."

"And staying with him will probably break yours."

I threw her a sharp glare, which she batted away with a raise of her eyebrows.

"I know you're a sweet soul, but that doesn't

always serve you well. A little pain and angst now might just save your life." Morgan ended the conversation with a pointed look, sliding on her coat and walking toward the door.

I swallowed and slowly turned to follow her, snatching up my own jacket and pulling it on in robotic motion.

It felt selfish to put my heart before David's, but was Morgan right? Would I end up becoming some bitter woman if I stayed with him? Would we grow old together, David blissfully unaware of my heartache and me retracting into a turtle mode so deep no one would ever be able to pull me free?

Locking our door, I caught up with Morgan down the corridor. She put her arm around my shoulders and gave me a little squeeze. I could tell she wanted to say more but mercifully kept her lips sealed as we walked into the cool night air. A light rain descended from the bleak sky. David was waiting for me at the car, his eyes lighting with admiration. He held an umbrella over me as I approached.

I greeted him with a kiss that he leaned away from because he didn't want to get lipstick on his face. It ended up being an air kiss against his cheek. With a false smile, I slid into the car. His arm dropped over my shoulder as he directed the driver to where we were headed and I prepared myself for another night of fake smiles and forced enthusiasm.

I had spent most of my teenage life trying to avoid these feelings of isolation and vulnerability, but as I sat in my boyfriend's arms listening to his giddy excitement, they swamped over me, weighing me down until I thought I might suffocate.

THIRTY-TWO
COLE

I got to the party before David. I'd promised him I'd get there early to make sure the set-up was perfect. David's brother Luke arrived about ten minutes after me, and we spent the early evening talking to the caterers and setting up the microphone for the speeches. The room looked good. Plain, white, simple. Just the way David liked it.

Leaning against the bar, I nursed my bottle of beer and watched David's law buddies slowly filter in. He'd invited every single one of his Chicago friends, and the room was soon filled with nearly a hundred people. This night was going to suck.

I picked at the label on my bottle and waited, my eyes trained on the door. She was going to walk through any second, and it would be the first time I'd seen her since last weekend.

Her kiss still buzzed on my lips. The feeling was fading, but if I closed my eyes and relived it, it was right there again, injecting a liquid fire into my limbs and making my insides tremble.

I had so badly wanted to tell her about David's plans. I'd nearly called her twice, and I'd actually been at her door one afternoon, ready to knock, but I just couldn't do it. David made me promise, and I never broke those lightly. To say I was nervous about how she'd react was an understatement. Asking her in front of all these people would no doubt force a yes. Was that David's plan? He was a master manipulator; not in a cruel way, just in *the guy knew how to get what he wanted* way. He was always nice about it, and I was sure he had no idea he was doing it half the time.

I wondered if that was how he'd managed to keep Ella close for so long. His words held a magical quality that could elicit just the right emotion at just the right time. Would she have the strength to stand up to it?

I closed my eyes.

No. She wouldn't.

Taking a swig, I continued to pick at the label with my thumb until I caught a flash of bright pink. My body jerked, my hand squeezing the bottle so tight I thought the glass might shatter.

Damn, she was beautiful.

She looked my way, her eyes brushing over mine. I saw the tendons in her neck ping tight as she jerked her head in the opposite direction. Her fingers squeezed David's hand and he gazed down at her, his smile sweet and mushy. She grinned back at him, and I knew my days were done.

She was going to say yes. She was going to pretend she'd never heard my voice, never felt my touch, and never helped me build my dreams. She was going to deny it all out of some sick loyalty.

I turned my back to her, unable to look. I was tempted to skulk out of the room and not return, but I couldn't ditch my friend. I'd never be able to explain myself.

"Cole! Hey, man!" David walked across the room toward me. I spun to face him and wrapped him in a half hug, banging his back.

"Happy birthday."

"Thanks." He chuckled. "Should be a good night."

"Yeah, definitely." I glanced across the room at Ella.

"She has no idea." David grinned. "That hot young thing over there is going to be one happy woman by the end of the evening."

I wanted to punch the arrogant smirk off his lips, but instead forced a chuckle from my throat. "You're a lucky man."

"That I am." He slapped my back one more time and then moved away to greet other guests. I decided to stay by the bar. People could come to me tonight. I didn't think my legs could carry me around the room anyway.

*****

I slumped back in my seat, ignoring the delicious slice of cheesecake placed before me. It looked so good, but I just couldn't touch it. Luke's speech was making everyone crow with laughter.

I could barely muster a grin.

David invited me to sit at their table for dinner, and it was more than awkward. Ella and I both tried our best, put on a show that Morgan could see right through. Her gaze kept flickering between us. David was in his storytelling form, which thankfully made him oblivious to the tension around him. Whenever his brows started to furrow or his eyes narrowed at the corners, one of us would say something light or crack a joke, killing the suspicion. To me, it looked ridiculously dubious, but David was onto his third beer already, and his inebriated state was making him just a little less sharp.

Luke rounded off his speech with some touching words about his baby brother. Everybody murmured their approval before breaking into applause.

I took the opportunity to slip from my seat and head over to the bar. Luke was inviting his brother to stand and I wanted to throw up. Maybe I should get off-my-ass drunk. I could wake up in the morning and not remember any of this damn night, but I knew I couldn't do it. I needed to be alert for what was to come.

I knew it was an insane move, but for some reason I was compelled to let Ella shatter my heart into a thousand pieces. It felt like the only real way to get over her.

David grabbed the microphone and pushed his chair back.

"Thank you so much, everyone. This has been an awesome night, and I feel so honored to have you all here with me. I couldn't have asked for a better twenty-first party." He smiled around the room and then looked down at Ella.

My stomach coiled into a tight knot.

"But the main person I want to thank tonight is my gorgeous girl, Ella. Stand up, baby."

Her smile faltered as she gathered her napkin and placed it on the table. The last thing she wanted to do was stand, but she capitulated, tucking a lock of hair behind her ear and looking down at the table.

"Ella, baby." David took her hand and forced her to face him. "I love you."

She swallowed, nerves skittering over her expression.

"Everyone knows I want to spend the rest of my life with you."

Her smile was tight until David reached into his pocket and pulled out that wretched black box. Her mouth dropped open, her eyelashes flying high.

I swallowed, turning away from the scene.

"I know we were gonna wait until after I graduated, but I don't think I can hold out that long."

I turned back in time to see David drop to his knee. Excited gasps rippled through the room. I caught Morgan's tense expression out of the corner of my eye, but as soon as my gaze landed on Ella's pale face, I couldn't take my eyes off her.

"Ella, will you marry me?"

David popped the lid, revealing the sparkling diamond. She glanced at it and swallowed, panic flittering over her expression. My eyebrows bunched together and I leaned forward as her gaze shot across the room and landed straight on me. The desperation in her eyes sparked a glimmer of hope. I stood from my seat, my mouth agape.

She looked away from me, back to David, her quivering lips rising with a smile.

"Um..." Her chuckle was nervous as she ran a finger over her ear, tucking away a nonexistent lock of hair.

David's grip on her hand grew a little tighter, his head tipping to the side. "Baby?"

"Ah..." Her breaths were coming out punchy and she looked ready to pass out.

David stood, his expression knotting in confusion. "Why aren't you saying yes?"

"I'm, uh...just surprised. I thought we were

gonna wait." She swallowed, trying for a brave smile, but she couldn't quite muster one.

David loomed over her, making her look small and fragile. His jaw worked to the side as he coughed out a laugh. "What's the point of waiting if we know it's what we want?"

Ella's mouth worked like a goldfish. She stared up at him, scratching the back of her neck and running her hand over her shoulder. "Well, I...I don't...."

"You don't what?" David's razor-sharp tone cut straight through her, and I had to force my feet to remain planted.

Leaning toward him, she went on her tiptoes to whisper, but the microphone caught her soft words and pushed them into the room. "Can we talk about this privately?"

"No, no we can't." David threw his arms wide and stepped back from her. "Everyone here was expecting you to say yes, so I think we're all pretty interested in why you're not doing that right now."

His loud voice riled me. Anger coursed through my system, and I wasn't the only one. I could see Morgan's nostrils flaring. Everyone else in the room was looking down at their plates or throwing wide-eyed glances at each other.

Ella was getting desperate, but it was too late for her now. It wasn't like she could just slap him on the chest and say, "Kidding!"

Everyone in the room would smell the lie.

"Please, David." Ella bit her lip. "Don't do this."

"I'm not the one doing anything wrong here." He shrugged, snapping the ring box closed and throwing it onto the table. It clattered against the cutlery and Brad only just saved a wine glass from spilling over.

Ella flinched.

David turned to the room with a snigger,

rubbing the back of his neck before turning back to Ella. "I propose to my girlfriend of three years, who I am in love with, expecting her to say yes and she's not, so where am I at fault here?"

She swallowed, rolling her shoulder and gripping her hands together.

"So it's no then?" David bent down to her level. "Which obviously means you want to break up with me."

Her wide-eyed fear screamed a loud yes. Anyone watching her could see the answer clearly on her face.

David let out another bewildered laugh. "You're breaking up with me at my twenty-first birthday party. Nice."

His sarcastic tone made me want to punch him. What the hell was he doing?

"I didn't know you were gonna propose," Ella replied softly.

"Oh, so you were just stringing me along then?"

"David, come on, man. That's enough." Luke touched his shoulder, but David flicked him off, kicking his chair out of the way and keeping his hard gaze on Ella.

"Don't hurt the boy on his birthday. That's what you were thinking, right? It's better to wait." He shook his head with a sardonic laugh. "You know I have a huge test in a couple of days, maybe you could break up with me then. Or we could wait until Christmas, so my parents could be there too."

Luke righted the fallen chair, ready to step in again.

Ella stepped toward him, raising her hand to try to calm him down. "David, please stop. I'm sorry, okay, but I can't say yes." Her voice held more strength than I was expecting it to. "I didn't want to hurt you, and I'm sorry for...I'm sorry."

"Get out." David sniffed.

Ella's head jerked back, confusion scoring her features.

"Can we talk about this, please? I really—"

"Get out!" David leaned forward, screaming the words in her face and pointing at the door.

Ella stumbled back, her butt hitting the table. Glasses trembled, two of them falling over and splashing red wine across the white tablecloth. Morgan stood from her seat, firing an angry glare at David while reaching for Ella. Her hand skimmed Ella's shoulder, but the petite girl flinched and flicked her off, grabbing her purse and racing from the room.

There was a pregnant minute of awkward silence before the whispers started. David paced the edge of the room like a raging bull while Luke tried to stand in his path and calm him. I knew I should have probably headed over there and checked in, but instead, I followed Morgan as she chased after Ella.

I ran into the hotel lobby and pushed through the revolving door. Morgan stood at the curb, rain soaking into her dress as she yelled to the taxi that was driving away.

"She's gone?"

"Yeah." Morgan pointed at the departing cab.

"Can I go after her?" The question came out of nowhere. I had no idea I was going to say it, but now that I had, it was all I wanted.

Morgan looked at me. "Are you sure that's the best idea?"

I lifted my shoulders, letting out a sigh. "I just need to make sure she's okay."

Morgan's sharp gaze softened, a small smile cresting over her lips. "You know what, you might be exactly what she needs tonight."

Morgan pushed Ella's coat into my hands and stepped back. "Call me if she needs me."

I nodded, my throat too clogged to speak.

Ella had said no. She'd looked me straight in the eye and then turned back to David and said no.

Raising my arm, I tried to hail a taxi. It took ten minutes and three attempts before one finally stopped for me. Saturated, I ran toward it, rattling off the address before I'd even closed the door.

Leaning back against the leather, I relived the scene, hating the way David spoke to her, but loving the way she stood her ground. Ella had said no.

I flicked the raindrops off my face and couldn't help a smile.

THIRTY-THREE
ELLA

By the time I reached my dorm suite, I was a soaking-wet, quivering mess. Pulling at the pink straps of my dress, I wriggled out of the wet material and threw it on the floor. I slashed at the tears on my icy face, no doubt smudging mascara everywhere. I didn't care.

I'd never seen David so riled before. The way he screamed at me to get out...I sniffed, slipping into my room to find a Kleenex. My heart felt fractured and sore.

Yanking at my shoes, I flicked them off my toes and grabbed a handful of tissue, dabbing at my puffing eyes.

In spite of the intense pain emanating from my chest, there was a whistle of freedom singing through fracture lines. I felt bad for the glimmer of hope. I didn't really deserve it, but part of me wanted to let out a war cry.

Hurting David was a wound to myself, but when I saw Cole's aching gaze on me, I couldn't say yes. Morgan was right. I didn't want David's dreams anymore...I wanted my own. All I needed to do now was figure out what they were.

Pulling out a T-shirt, I slipped it over my bra and panties, hugging the cotton fabric around me. David's eyes had been molten with rage. It seemed so out of character for him to humiliate me...and himself...in front of everyone like that.

I stopped, my arms dropping to my sides as a thought occurred to me.

Me not saying yes was the first time things hadn't gone to plan for him. When it came to me, he was used to getting his way. Everything was laid out for him, his vision was clear, and I'd just pooed all over it.

I squeezed my eyes shut and rubbed my temples.

He'd never forgive me for this.

David was a strong man, and he was used to getting what he wanted.

I sniffed again, stretching my neck tall and reminding myself I'd done the right thing.

Needing a distraction, I snatched the remote off my desk and pointed it at the stereo. I had no idea what playlist was currently on my iPod, but strains of jazz and blues filtered through the speakers, and I was soon listening to "Stormy Weather."

I rolled my eyes and pressed fast forward.

"Cry Me a River" began. I was about to press fast forward again but then dropped the remote on my desk. All I felt like doing was crying a river; it was the perfect song for my mood.

I slumped onto my bed, resting my elbows on

my knees and scraping my fingers through my knotty, wet hair.

In spite of the fact I'd done the right thing, fear still coursed through me. Could I handle the aftermath of my decision?

A knock sounded at my door.

I sat up, a breath spurting out of my nose as dread rippled down my spine. Was it David? Had he come to dish out more?

Closing my eyes, I drooped my head and knew I couldn't ignore it. If it was David, we'd just have to talk it out. I knew he'd try to convince me to rethink my decision, but now that I'd rejected him once, I knew I couldn't go back. This was the start of something new for me, and even though it was hell-scary, I had to keep pressing forward.

Shuffling to the door, I touched the handle and drew in a breath of courage. The person rapped on the door one more time and I pulled it open, the air in my lungs evaporating as I looked into Cole's blue eyes and felt my insides sizzle.

"Hey." His smile was soft and gentle. His lips barely moved, but his gaze grew warm with compassion, making me want to cry again. "I just wanted to make sure you were okay."

He held out my jacket and I took it from him, throwing it onto the desk beside me.

I opened my mouth to say I was fine, but I wasn't. Not with him standing there, turning my legs to toothpaste and my brain to melted butter. He was so damn sexy; he had no idea. His wet shirt was plastered to his body, his dark curls glistening. Droplets ran down his face. I wanted to lick them off his smooth skin. The very idea made me dizzy.

I glanced to the floor, clutching the door for support and scolding my wicked mind.

"I can go if you want me to," Cole whispered.

My gaze flew up from the floor and our eyes

locked...like they had on the dance floor, and I knew it wasn't just my feverish body that made me want Cole.

I was in love with him.

I was in love with the way he made me feel. I was in love with the fact that he knew me. He'd seen the real me, something I hardly ever showed a soul.

He was my Prince Charming, the one who would dance me off into the sunset.

My inner revelation froze me still. I'd been holding it at bay, shoving it aside with thoughts of David, but right now there was no David. There was just me and Cole...and I really did love him.

He leaned his arm against the doorframe, staring down at me, waiting for me to invite him in or send him on his way.

And there was only one thing I could do.

My body took over before my brain even moved. Stretching to my tiptoes, I wrapped my fingers around the back of his neck and crushed my lips to his. He jerked with surprise then melted against me, his large hands fluttering over my ribs and running down to my waist. He felt divine, perfect, and I didn't care what consequences followed. All I wanted to do was make love to him and forget the rest of the world existed.

As if reading my mind, my shuffle switched to Etta James's "I Just Want To Make Love To You." Giggles rippled through my stomach but didn't have time to form as Cole stepped further into the room and flicked the door closed with his foot. His hands slid over my hips, flicking my shirt out of the way so he could cup my butt. With one swift move, he lifted me into his arms. I rested my forearms on his shoulders, running my fingers into his curls and devouring him with hot kisses. Our lips hadn't parted since I first reached for him, my body turning into an inferno with each slip of his tongue.

A soft moan reverberated from his throat as I squeezed my legs around him, pressing my pulsing body against his wet torso. Pushing me against the wall, his lips moved from my mouth to my throat. Closing my eyes, I tipped my head back, savoring each nip and lick.

This was like nothing I'd ever experienced before. His free hand snaked beneath my shirt, wriggling north until it found my lacy bra, his firm fingers undoing me quickly as he gently squeezed and brushed my nipple.

I gripped his shoulders, groaning with pleasure as his lips worked over my collarbone and tried to gain access to the rest of my skin. Panting like I'd just run five miles, I grappled with my shirt, pulling it over my head and throwing it across the room. His deep chuckle made my skin prickle as he looked up at me. I touched his face, my insides swelling with affection. I wanted to whisper that I loved him, but I couldn't speak.

His gaze was an intense mix of passion and magic. It's like he knew what I was thinking and felt exactly the same way. I brushed my teeth over my bottom lip, running my fingers down his chiseled jawline. Michelangelo had carved him from marble, and I couldn't wait to run my fingers over the rest of his perfect form.

My heart rate accelerated with the idea, my fingers tugging at his shirt. As I worked at his buttons, he carried me to my room and sat on the edge of the bed. I freed the last button and whipped off his shirt and jacket together. He flicked them off his wrists, his hands back on me in a second. They deftly undid my bra while I ran my hands over his granite frame. The curve of his muscles made my fingertips sizzle. As soon as my bra hit the floor, I slid toward him, pressing our naked bodies together and sighing into his mouth.

This was heaven.

I stretched my neck back as his lips urged me to lean away from him. In one smooth move, he shifted me from his lap to the bed. As his lips worked over my breasts, his fingers traveled up my thighs, slipping under my panties and sparking something inside me that was tantalizing and new. He helped me wriggle out of the material and went back to business, his scintillating touch making me whimper. I gripped a handful of his hair as his tongue and fingers cast a spell on my body.

I swear I reached a higher plane as he brought me to a climax that rippled through my body in waves so strong, my back arched and I ended crying out his name. My body felt limp as I fell back to the bed, but it was still burning hot and I reached for his pants, unwrapping my prize with a smile.

He groaned at my touch, closing his eyes and resting his forehead against mine. He looked into my eyes, pausing and pulling away from my arching hips. It was a sweet torture as he brushed a lock of hair off my face and opened his mouth to whisper something.

But his words were stolen by a new song floating into the room. Our bodies both quivered with laughter as Louis Armstrong began "Cheek to Cheek" in his gravelly voice.

I touched Cole's face, my expression softening as we relived our first connection. This was the shower song that had changed my life forever.

Cole's smile was delicious as he slipped inside me. My breath caught, followed by a sweet gasp of pleasure. I tipped my head back and ran my hand up his arm, scraping my nails lightly over his shoulders. I could feel his gaze on me as his fingers whispered over my skin.

I looked up at him, matching his steady rhythm and getting lost in his gaze. We drank each other in until my body was tingling right down to my toes, and I had to arch my neck back into the pillow. His lips trailed over my exposed skin and his pace grew quick. His light fingers became firm as he lifted my thigh, burying himself inside of me. My heel skimmed his hard buttocks and I pressed myself against his every move, wanting to meld my body with his.

Our breathing accelerated, in time with each other, as we crested the high point of our wave and both tumbled over the edge in a limbless spiral that had me seeing stars. He squeezed my thigh and moaned into my neck. My arms dropped from his shoulders, feeling like pieces of loose string, and I let out a luxurious sigh.

Propping himself up on his elbows, Cole studied me with his bright blue eyes then placed a sweet kiss on my nose, followed by a warm kiss to my lips.

It was a perfect moment and one I would cling to forever.

THIRTY-FOUR

COLE

When Ella first opened the door to me in nothing but a T-shirt, I thought my body might combust. Her tear-streaked face was smudged black with mascara, her hazel eyes bright from crying, but she was beautiful.

I never expected her to reach for me, but as soon as she did, I couldn't hold back.

I'd just had the most amazing sex of my life.

A smile spread over my lips as I relived the midnight hours. We'd explored each other's bodies thoroughly, catching short bursts of sleep in between the fire. I felt spent, yet euphoric.

Rolling over with a soft moan, I reached for her, wanting to wrap my arm around her. Her soft breast fit perfectly inside my hand last night, her butt resting against my torso and igniting new sparks of flame. My body responded just thinking about her.

My hand traveled over the bed, and I opened my eyes. She was gone.

Propping up on my elbow, I glanced around the room and found her resting against the doorframe, gazing at me with a look of longing and agony.

It unsettled me, but I put on a smile anyway. Damn she looked hot, standing there in nothing but a tank top and panties. I couldn't wait to rip those things off her again.

"Come back to bed, birdy."

She grinned at the nickname I'd given her sometime during the night. We'd laughed and kissed, which had then turned into a heated reconnection that was fast and slick. I felt like I'd made love to her in every way I could throughout the night, and I was looking forward to a slow, luxurious repeat this morning.

I patted the bed and arched my eyebrows, but she shook her head.

Her smile was sad as she looked down at her fidgeting fingers. "We can't do this, Cole."

I tried not to let the statement terrify me, but it did. My lips stretched with a lopsided grin. "I think we already did."

"But we shouldn't have." She closed her eyes with a shaky laugh and leaned her head against the wood. The muscles on her face strained tight, and I knew the next time she looked at me, there'd be tears in her eyes.

Keeping my voice calm was an effort, but I slowly sat up, my gaze trained on her face. "You broke up with him, Ella."

"And five minutes later, I was sleeping with you!" Her eyes flew open, shining with tears. "What we did last night was..."

"Amazing."

Her breath hitched, her shoulders slumping as heat rose over her cheeks. Pressing her lips together, she crossed her arms and pulled her body straight. "It was wrong. What we did was wrong."

Shit!

"I'm gonna have to disagree with you on that one." I couldn't keep the clip from my voice. Throwing back the covers, I grabbed my pants off the floor and threw my legs into them. Zipping the fly, I walked toward her. I wanted my words to sound as sincere as I felt, so I kept my voice soft. "Last night was right in every way for me."

I touched her face, running my thumb over her cheekbone and tucking my fingers behind her neck. I could feel her flimsy resolve crumbling and moved further into her space. Her breath whispered against my skin. I drew my lips to hers, brushing my tongue lightly over her soft mouth.

She responded immediately, her body melting against mine, our hot hungry tongues dancing together. I ran my hands down her body, ready to lift her into my arms again, but she pulled away from me with a sob.

Holding her mouth, she ducked under my arm and stumbled into the living room.

"He's your best friend, Cole!"

The words were like darts through my chest. I gripped the wooden frame in front of me and wanted to smash my head against it.

"You are more important to me than my friendship with him."

"You can't just throw it all away. I won't let you do it." She spun to face me, tears now streaming unchecked over her perfect cheeks.

I was in front of her in two steps, gently pinching her chin between my thumb and forefinger. Our eyes locked together, I made sure of that, following her darting gaze until she had to give in and stare straight at me.

"I know it's complicated, and I'm not saying it's gonna be easy, but I love you."

A soft smile brushed her lips.

"I've never said that to a girl before, so I know I mean it, Ella. I am seriously in love with you, and I know you feel the same way."

Her smile faltered, a frown cresting over her face.

"You have to do what's right for you. Don't think about David."

She stepped out of my grasp, and I had to let her go. It killed me to just stand there, watching her dig a chasm between us.

"So, what was last night then?" I put my hands on my hips, unable to hold back my spark of desperate anger. "Just a little fun before you dump me and run back to him?"

"No! Of course not! It was never just about fun for me." Her eyes were wide with anguish and I had to believe her. "Last night will be a perfect moment in my life...one I'm never gonna forget."

"Please don't talk like that." My voice hitched. "We can make this work. David will come around eventually. It might take time, but if we're patient, we can—"

"I can't, Cole." She raised her hand. "It's not just about David. I need..." Her mouth moved, but no words came forth. I wanted to step in and fill the space with logic and argument, but my throat was clogged.

She dropped her chin to her chest and let out a shaky breath. "I'm sorry, but I can't be with you right now."

My heart cracked as she looked up at me. Her tears were as soul-destroying as her words. I shook my head, gently moving toward her.

"Ella, please don't do this." I reached for her hands and she let me take them. Closing my eyes, I pressed my lips against the top of her head. I knew she wanted me. I knew she was putting David before us, and I couldn't let that happen.

"Let me go and talk to him. We'll sort this out, it'll be okay." I squeezed her fingers when she shook her head, but I couldn't listen. I was too fueled by the thought of talking David around. If we could convince him to be cool with this, it'd all be okay.

I rushed to grab my stuff, throwing on my shirt and haphazardly doing up the buttons.

She hadn't said anything, just watched me with a look of desolation.

I ignored it. I had to.

Bending down, I placed a kiss on her lips. "I'll be back."

I rushed for the door before she could say anything else. I thought I heard her whisper something, but I didn't know what she said. I had another confrontation I needed to psych myself up for. It wouldn't be pretty, but I'd do whatever it took to keep Ella.

THIRTY-FIVE

ELLA

"I won't be here." I whispered the words as Cole swung the door shut. He didn't hear me and that was okay. I knew I had to leave.

Last night was magic, heaven...perfection.

But it had to be a one-time thing.

Life wasn't always roses and cupcakes, and as much as I wanted Cole, he couldn't be my Prince Charming.

We didn't have a sunset.

We had reality. We had David.

What were we supposed to do, just start going out as if the guy didn't exist anymore? It couldn't work and I couldn't stay; the fallout from my decision last night was too monumental. It scared the shit out of me and I had to get away.

The idea of being on my own was less terrifying than facing the conflict ahead.

Running back to my room, I snatched out a pair of jeans and pulled them on. Grabbing out a T-shirt, I threw it over my tank top and shimmied into my sweater and jacket. I yanked the backpack out from under my bed and began haphazardly throwing things inside, trying to get my frantic brain to think through what I'd need.

There was no folding involved. I just dumped things randomly inside, the bag getting heavier with each item. Dropping it onto my tussled sheets, I felt my fractured heart splintering a little more.

I ran my fingers over my pillow and remembered, my eyes closing as the sweet ecstasy of my night permeated the corners of my brain.

A sob burst from between my lips and I sniffed. Tears exploded from my eyes as I grabbed my round packet of pills off my bedside table. I popped one into my mouth and swallowed it down, wondering if I'd ever need birth control again.

How would any man ever measure up to Cole? He was magic and passion wrapped up in one. He was my perfect match. If I walked away from him now, I knew I was sealing my fate. I would be single for the rest of my life. But I had to go. I just knew I had to go.

Zipping my bag closed, I wiped my sleeve over my face and headed for the door.

It swung open before I got to it, and I dropped my bag in fright.

Breathing out a sigh of relief, I looked at Morgan, a fresh wave of tears coursing down my face.

"What happened?"

I shook my head, swiping at tears and trying to rein in my punchy breaths.

"Did Cole find you?"

"He spent the night," I hiccupped.

Morgan's eyes lit up and she closed the door before turning to me with a smile. "I thought he might. That's why I chose to stay at Brad's. How was it?"

"How do you think it was?" I threw my hands in the air. "It was freaking amazing, Morgan!"

Her face crested with a compassionate smile. "So, if it was so great, why do you look like you're about to shatter?"

"It can't work." I shrugged. "How could it ever work? I can't screw up their friendship. I'm not gonna be the girl they fight over."

"Honey, Cole is so perfect for you. You're seriously just gonna leave him? I thought you loved him."

"I do. You have no idea how much." I shook my head, pressing my lips together as my tummy trembled. "But I have to go. I have to figure out what's right for me, and I can't do that around him. I can't be this close to David and Cole...and even you! I need some space...on my own to work this all out."

Morgan paused, her eyes darting to the floor before settling on me. Her smile was beaming with pride. "Good girl." She nodded. "I've been wanting you to say that for a long time."

I rushed into her arms and pressed my face against her shoulder. "I'm petrified."

She squeezed me tight. "You're stronger than you think, and once you've had some space to breathe, you'll know. You'll know what's worth fighting for."

She pushed me away from her and held me at arm's length. "Where are you gonna go?"

"I don't know yet. I just can't be here."

"Do you want me to take you anywhere?"

"No, I'm gonna head to the bus station and decide from there."

She looked worried but put on a brave face. "Promise you'll call me once you're settled. Jody will freak out if she doesn't know where you are."

I grinned. I knew she really meant her. "I will." I gripped her elbows. "Promise you won't tell Cole once you know."

Her expression faltered, bunching with reluctance before finally relaxing. "Are you sure?"

No, of course I wasn't sure! It hurt like hell to think he could never find me, but I knew he'd follow me and if he did, I wouldn't be able to resist him.

"Promise me, Morgan."

She sighed and gave a stiff nod. "I promise."

"Thank you."

I stepped into her embrace again, clinging to her. It was like saying goodbye to my mother in some ways, and it tore me apart. Tears shook out of me and it took every ounce of willpower to step out of her grasp.

"Be safe," she whispered.

"I will." I nodded back, clicking the door open.

I stepped into the corridor, clutching the bag tightly in my hand. My old friends, vulnerability and isolation, sat heavy on my shoulders, turning my legs to lead, but I fought them all the way. Keeping my eyes straight ahead, I walked out of the building, away from the people I loved.

As I raised my arm to hail the passing taxi, I felt a small flutter of freedom rush through me, like in spite of this pain I was somehow doing the right thing.

I slid into the cab and pressed my head back into the seat.

"Where to, lady?"

"The Greyhound bus station, please."

He pulled away from the curb and I closed my eyes, tears silently falling once again as I drove away from the best thing that had ever happened to me.

THIRTY-SIX
COLE

I didn't know if I'd find David in our room or not, but that was where I started.

"David! You in here, man?" My heart was hammering as I flicked the door closed behind me.

I knew my night with Ella had been every kind of right, but I also felt like a scummy friend. Sure, they'd broken up, but Ella was right...there had been zero grace period.

I wanted to scold myself for crossing a line, but I just couldn't. Ella in my arms had been perfection, and I needed more of her...for the rest of my life.

"Dave-o?" I glanced into his room. His bed was still neatly made, meaning he probably hadn't made it home.

I spun to leave and then heard a soft groan from

the couch.

Peering over the cushions, I spotted his arm dangling to the floor. I could smell the alcohol wafting off him and wrinkled my nose.

"David." I slapped his back.

He groaned again and slowly pushed himself up. His bleary eyes studied me slowly before he leaned back against the couch and sighed.

"How you doin', man?" My initial urge was to take a seat beside him and hear him out, but I was a little tentative to get within range.

Shoving my hands in my pockets, I stood on the other side of the couch as he spun to look at me.

"How the fuck do you think I'm doing?"

Guilt singed my insides.

"I'm really sorry, man. I know it sucks for you."

He scoffed, rubbing a hand over his face. "So, where the hell have you been? I saw you chasing Ella out the door." His tone was brittle. "I don't suppose she got run over by a taxi, did she?"

My frown was sharp and disapproving. "Don't talk like that, man."

He glared at me. "Where were you? Were you with her?"

I swallowed, wanting to lie, deny my actions, but what was the point? I wanted to be with Ella and that meant telling the truth to her ex-boyfriend. I let out a sigh and looked to the ground. "Yeah, man. I was with her."

"What?" David's head snapped up and he jumped from the couch. His gaze was now razor sharp, and he looked like he wanted to rip my head off.

I raised my hands and backed away from him.

"You were with her? Like all night?"

I swallowed.

His jaw clenched, his neck muscles straining tight as he pointed at me. "Man, you better have just been talking."

I kept my gaze steady, telling him the truth without saying a word.

His face blanched, his lips bunching tight.

"I love her. I'm sorry, man. I never meant for it to happen, but from the second I met her, I—"

"You fucked my girlfriend?"

"No!" My voice was firm. The very idea of anyone fucking Ella made my skin crawl. I'd made love to her, cherished every inch of her precious skin and told her in a thousand different ways just what she meant to me.

I wanted to rip David's head off for even saying it.

Swallowing back my rage, I forced my voice to remain calm. "She's not your girlfriend anymore. You broke up."

"Last night! We broke up last night!" He practically screamed the words as his arms flung wide. "What the fuck, Cole! You're my best friend! How long have you two been sneaking around behind my back?"

"Ella never cheated on you. The first time we were together was last night. We have been fighting this for months."

"Oh, well, thank you for your consideration. You're such a good friend, man." His scathing tone felt like talons clawing over my exposed skin.

"We didn't mean for this to happen. Sometimes you can't control these things. Ella—"

"Oh yes, Ella, the perfect angel." He spat the word.

"David, she's amazing."

"I know!" His voice cracked, his hurt finally showing through his anger.

His pain punctured through me, but I had to keep going. I had to make him see that this was right; not just for her, but for him, too.

"Do you? Do you really know how awesome she is?"

"What the hell is that supposed to mean?"

"I just..." I sighed. "You've been so focused on your plan and what you want that I don't think you realize how different you and Ella really are."

David's glare turned into a molten look that made my stomach quake. I knew I was bigger than my roommate, and if he tried to attack me, I could probably come out of the fight triumphant. But he looked feral right now, and it was making me nervous.

I raised my palms to him and took another step back.

"Do you know she likes to dance? And she can sing." I couldn't help smiling. "Man, she sounds like an angel when she sings. Have you ever heard her?"

Breaths spurted through his nostrils, warning me he was a bull about to charge.

"I'm not trying to piss you off, man. I'm just trying to say that maybe this break-up is a blessing in disguise. Take me out of this equation and just ask yourself if you two were really right for each other."

"I'm gonna fucking kill you." He leapt over the couch with a war cry and dove toward me with his fist raised. I blocked the first blow with my forearm, but let him have a few free swings. I deserved it.

His knuckles crunched into my face, and I gritted my teeth against the pain. He wanted to pummel the living shit out of me, and part of me wanted to let him do it, but if Ella saw us like this, it'd just drive her further away. I had to calm things down.

We were on the floor now, rolling over each other and trying to get the upper hand. David pressed his hand into my chest and pushed me into the floor, punching my cheekbone. It frickin' hurt and I could see his reddened knuckles as he pulled back for another shot. I grabbed his fist and pushed it away from me, deciding enough was enough. With a roar, I shoved him back, jumping up before he could dive on me again.

"Enough!" I yelled, raising my hands, but he just kept coming.

Ducking to the side, I let him stumble past me and then jumped up behind him, wrapping my arm around his neck.

"Enough, man," I spoke into his ear.

He struggled against me, kicking and trying to break free, but my grip was tight. It took him a few minutes of fighting to figure it out, but eventually he sagged against me.

"All right, let me go!"

I tentatively loosened my grip and stepped back from him.

"Dav—"

"Shut up! You asshole! You fucking asshole!" His words were crushing, but I stood tall against them. "I don't ever want to see your face again." His finger shook as he pointed at me.

"Come on, David, please...we're not trying to hurt you. Ella doesn't want to be with me until we can resolve this. Think about what's best for her."

"Keep talking and you won't have any teeth left by the time I'm done."

I clenched my jaw and looked to the ground, knowing when to call it quits. "I'll move out today."

David grabbed his crumpled jacket off the end of the couch and flicked it out. "You better be gone by the time I get back this afternoon."

"Where are you going?"

"Why the hell do you care?"

"I care, man."

"Yeah, obviously." He shoved my shoulder as he walked past, nearly knocking me from my feet. The door slammed shut behind me and I flinched.

Tears burned my eyes, but I held them in check.

Now was not the time to fall apart.

I needed to see Ella, let her know what happened. She'd hate it, but I had to let her in. Truth would always be first place in our relationship, and I needed to start things on the right foot. I had no idea how she'd react.

Glancing at my room, I quickly calculated how long it would take me to box up my stuff. I'd have to call Malachi and ask if I could move back in. I knew it wouldn't be a problem, but I dreaded the call. Checking my watch, I made a beeline for Ella's room.

As soon as I told her, I'd head back and say goodbye to dorm living.

My hands were shaking as I rapped on the wood.

Morgan pulled the door open a few seconds later. Her eyes rounded when she looked at my face. I touched my aching cheek and winced. I'd forgotten I probably looked like an MMA fighter. I grimaced.

"I gotta talk to her."

Morgan gave me a sad smile. "She's not here."

I frowned. "Where'd she go?"

"I don't know. She just left."

"What do you mean she just left? What...?" I shook my head, words failing me.

"I'm sorry, Cole, but she grabbed her stuff and took off."

"Her stuff? As in, all her stuff?"

"As much as she could carry."

My stomach coiled into a tight knot and I bent forward, leaning my arm against the doorframe.

"She can't just leave."

"She had to."

I looked up at Morgan's soft words.

"She needs to figure out exactly what she wants, and she can't do that around you." Morgan's lips slumped into a frown as she rubbed my shoulder. "I know she loves you and leaving is breaking her heart, but we have to let her go."

"Do you know where she's going?"

Morgan shook her head. I could see she hated this as much as I did. "I told her she had to call me when she got there."

"Will you let me know?"

Her face bunched with pain and she ran her fingers down her necklace, fidgeting with the pendant on the end of it. "She made me promise not to tell you. I'm so sorry, Cole."

"But..." I let out a breath, feeling desperate.

"It's gonna be okay."

"How?" I pressed my forehead against my arm. "I've just lost her."

"If she's meant to be yours, she'll come back to you."

My scoff was hard and wooden as I pushed off the doorframe. I gave Morgan one more broken look before slumping back to my room and boxing up my stuff.

Memories from my perfect night skittered through my brain as I threw my stuff together. Punching my mattress with an angry cry, I slumped onto the floor. I didn't want memories. I wanted the real thing; not just for a night, but every day for the rest of my whole damn life.

Swiping my finger under my nose, I looked to the ceiling.

Here I was, rejected once more.

Rejected and alone.

It was a depressing destiny, but somehow it felt

like mine.

THIRTY-SEVEN
ELLA

4 months later...

I jiggled the cranky lock on my front door and grunted. Kicking the bottom corner with the toe of my shoe, I felt the lock pop and pushed the door open with my shoulder. This place was falling apart, but I still smiled as I entered the room and dropped my bag on the two-seater dining table.

Slumping down on the lumpy couch with a sigh, I buried my head into the cushions and closed my eyes. I was tired, down to my very core. I was working my ass off trying to catch up after missing so much school. Bellevue College had accepted my application and let me start in the winter quarter. It'd given me time to find a job and move out of the Motel 6 I'd been staying in. Two days before classes began, I'd found this little apartment — a mother-in-law apartment, tacked onto the back of Mrs. Duffy's house. She was a widow of ten years and had just celebrated her seventy-fifth birthday.

Although a slight busybody, she was a kind heart and I really did love her. She had me over for dinner every Tuesday night for pot roast on the condition I'd fill her in on all my school gossip. There really wasn't much. I'd kept to myself mostly, happy to throw my energies into my studies and forget.

But I couldn't forget.

My eyes popped open, images of Cole dancing before me no matter where I looked. I could picture him walking through my door, shooting me a kind smile as he dumped his bag. He'd walk over to the couch and flop down beside me, his warm hand running up my thigh as he nuzzled my neck and asked me what we should do for dinner.

The dream evaporated with my sigh.

I wished they would just leave me alone, but as the months ticked by, they grew stronger.

I'd danced around my kitchen with his ghost, singing to Ella and Louis and hearing his voice join me. I wanted him. I wanted the life we could have had together, but it'd been four months now and I wasn't sure I could get it. Had he moved on? Would he even want me after skipping out on him like that?

And then there was the whole David thing.

I still felt guilty about that. Morgan had finally fessed-up about their fight and how Cole had moved out. I'd destroyed a friendship, and I wasn't sure I could ever get over that guilt...no matter how far I ran.

Four months ago, I'd boarded a bus to Washington State. I didn't know what had compelled me home, but the second I stepped into Bellevue, I knew I'd made the right choice. In spite of my constant tears and aching heart, I stuck it out, walking past my old house and school. Reliving precious memories that I'd kept on lockdown for so long.

It'd taken me three weeks to muster the courage to visit the cemetery. I hadn't stood before my parents' tombstones since their joint funeral. My legs had buckled as I remembered the dirt being thrown over their gleaming caskets and I crumbled to the wet grass, running my fingers over their engraved names and sobbing. A light patter of rain had fallen over me, and my tears had slowly ebbed. It was like they were crying with me, wishing they could have been there to solve my problems.

But they couldn't.

They weren't.

It was up to me.

The next day, I'd looked up community colleges in the area and filled in my application forms. I was doing it, standing on my own two feet and surviving just fine. I was proud of myself. I'd found a job at a music and movie shop in town. They sold second-hand CDs, books and DVDs. I was having fun listening to all the music and watching old movies. I worked most weekends and every Thursday night. My boss was a funny guy and had been the first person to make me laugh since leaving Chicago. He even invited me to join his daughter's community choir, so every Monday I spent my evening singing in the alto section and loving every second of it.

Yep, I was settled. I was proving to myself that being on my own didn't have to be a scary thing.

The only problem with this new set-up was that I was miserable. I liked what I was doing. I just hated the fact I had no one to share it with. My house of love was empty and cold. At the end of my day, I came home to nothing.

I missed Morgan and Jody. We tried to Skype weekly, but it wasn't the same. They were worried about me, and every conversation ended with me having to justify why I was drawing out my self-discovery.

I guess I was scared.

I had unfinished business to deal with, and I knew until I'd closed old wounds, I'd never be able to move forward.

Picking up my phone, I ran my thumb over the screen, knowing I should make the call. I'd wanted to do it for weeks now, dial him up and talk it through, bare my soul and hope for a good outcome.

But I didn't deserve it.

"You can't keep going like this." I sighed.

My screen went black, so I pushed the button again and checked the time, an idea fluttering through me.

The sun was setting a little later these days. If I left right now, I'd make it there and back before dark.

Rising from the couch before I could change my mind, I grabbed my keys and bike helmet.

I hadn't been able to afford a car, so now rode everywhere. It was a bit of a drag, but I was getting fit and that part felt good.

It took me fifteen minutes to reach the cemetery. I steered my bike left down the first lane and pulled it to a stop, resting it against a tree. Clicking off my helmet, I hung it over the handlebars and slowly approached their graves.

"Hey, guys." I rubbed my thighs and knelt to

the ground in front of them. "I know I don't usually come on a Wednesday night, and I promise I'll head home before it gets dark. I just..." I sighed. Sometimes I felt silly talking to two headstones, but it always surprised me how whenever I thought that, something would make me change my mind.

A light breeze whistled through the grass at my knees. I ran my hand over the soft blades and smiled. Maybe they were here listening to me.

"As you know, I've avoided dealing with some stuff. I told you how it all went down, but I guess I never admitted just how much Cole means to me." I blinked at my tears. "You guys were really in love. I remember recognizing that early on. I want a marriage like yours...I just wish I didn't want it with Cole." I raised my eyebrows, letting out a pitiful laugh. "I thought the out-of-sight, out-of-mind effect would kick in and I'd be able to move on, but he's just not leaving me. I miss him. I ache for the life we could have together."

I sniffed.

"I know there's only one thing I can do. I feel like it could give me closure and then I could move on, but I'm scared. I have no idea what he'll say to me or if he'll even hear me out. But I have to resolve this. It's eating me up constantly. So—" I took a breath. "I thought I'd come here and make the call with you guys for support."

I pulled out my phone, the grass tickling my ankles as if telling me to go for it. Pulling in a breath, I held it as I found the number and pressed the CALL button.

I hadn't spoken to him since everything fell apart. He tried to call me once, but I ignored it, spending the rest of the day in a flustered panic, wondering what he'd wanted to say to me.

"Hello." He answered the phone, his voice so familiar I couldn't help a smile. I could picture how he was standing, the look on his face. He was no doubt scowling and my belly trembled.

"Hey, David."

He didn't say anything. He was probably regretting the fact he'd responded to my call.

His silence was torture, but he hadn't hung up, so I pressed on. "I know you probably never want to speak to me again."

"What do you want, Ella?"

"I want to apologize."

He scoffed. "For sleeping with my best friend? Or breaking my heart in front of a room full of people?"

I pressed my lips together, his words stinging. Tears seared my vision, but I had to keep it together. This was the one and only time I'd be making this call, and I had to make it count.

"Actually, I'm more sorry for not being honest with you. When we first got together, you were like this rock that held me steady. You were so sure of yourself and what you wanted, and I clung to that. I thought I could follow you anywhere and you'd keep me safe. It didn't even occur to me that I might not want the same things as you. You meant safety to me, and that's all I thought I needed." I licked my lip. "When you first left L.A., I guess I got my first taste of life without you. I hated it at first, but then it got comfy and I started to believe in my own strength, but you'd been so good to me and I never wanted to hurt you. I thought when I got to Chicago everything would fall back into place. Your dreams would become mine, and we'd live happily ever after."

"I would have been a good husband to you." His voice was tight and strained; his wounds were still raw and I hated myself for it.

"Yeah, you would have." I nodded. "You would have tried really hard, and we probably would have survived, but..." I sighed, reminding myself to be honest and not just say what he wanted to hear. "I don't want to survive a marriage, David, I want to enjoy it."

David's sigh was heavy. I paused, giving him room to speak.

Finally he mumbled, "Yeah, I guess that's fair."

"I know I hurt you. I feel like I'm doing it right now and I wish I could take that back, but if I'd been honest from the beginning, then I never would have made such a mess of things. I'm so sorry for humiliating you at your party and for letting you down." My voice wobbled as tears crept over me, pricking my eyes and making them ache. "You don't ever have to forgive me for what happened, but I needed you to know how sorry I was. I've always been a coward. The idea of hurting you killed me, so I stayed silent and just made everything worse." I sucked in a shaky breath, sniffing and wiping at my tears.

"Where are you? What are you doing?" David's voice was soft, taking me by surprise.

I sniffed, sitting up a little straighter. "I'm uh... I'm at a little community college in Bellevue...Bellevue College." I chuckled. "In Washington."

"You went home. I thought you swore never to go back."

"Yeah, I thought it'd be too painful, but it's okay."

"Are you happy?"

"Yeah, yeah, pretty much. It's a good life. I feel proud of myself for being able to do this on my own. It's my first time that I've ever been independent and I needed to be, you know? So, yeah. Yeah, it's good."

"You miss Cole, don't you?"

He didn't sound angry, just really sad. My voice

caught in my throat, and I had to swallow twice before being able to speak.

"I never meant to fall in love with him, David, I swear. It just happened and I didn't have the strength to stop it. I tried. I really tried. That's why I had to walk away. I knew if I stayed I had to be with him, and I didn't want to hurt you even more."

"You left for me?" His voice rose with surprise.

"You make it sound like I never loved you."

"Did you?"

"Yes! David, you were my first love, and I will always be grateful that I had you in my life. Please, believe me. You were everything I needed when we first got together. I wanted us to last. I really did."

His silence was nerve-wracking. I wasn't sure if he believed me, and it hurt to think it.

"I guess I had to leave for myself as well. I had to get over you properly and figure out what my dreams looked like."

"What do they look like?"

"I'm still working on it." I smiled, not wanting to admit how heavily Cole played in all of them. "I'm taking a bunch of different classes at school, trying to figure out what interests me the most and what I want to do with my life."

"No more literature?"

I swallowed. "I do like reading, I just...those classes never really inspired me."

"Then why did you take them? Why did you let me push you in that direction?"

"Because I didn't know how to say no to you. I wanted to make you happy."

"No wonder we couldn't make it," he whispered, a bitterness giving his words a sharp edge.

I wanted to hang up the phone right then, guilt

making my heart race so fast I thought I might pass out.

"Why'd you really call me, Ella?"

"I needed closure. I needed you to hear the truth."

"You want my blessing, don't you?"

I nearly dropped the phone.

"Excuse me?"

"To be with Cole. You want me to tell you it's okay for you guys to be together."

"I...I would never expect that from you. That's not fair."

"But you want it."

"I...I..."

Did I?

Was that why I had called?

No. I shook my head. I didn't need David's permission. It was about apologizing. It was about closure!

"Ella?"

"I haven't called him. He doesn't even know where I am."

"I know." He snickered. "I find that kind of surprising actually. I thought you guys would be shacked up together in no time."

"I couldn't do that to you."

"So, once again, you're gonna let me steal all your dreams?"

My heart hitched. "David...I..."

"You made me happy. I loved being with you. You were the perfect girlfriend. You'd come when I'd call. You'd do anything for me. But you didn't want to be doing any of that stuff, did you? I thought I'd been making you happy, but it'd just been an act."

"You did make me happy. You—"

"I didn't. Not really and how was I even supposed to when you just went along with everything I said?"

"I was trying to be supportive."

"You wouldn't let me in, Ella. You lied."

My face dropped.

"I want to hate you for it. I never noticed that you weren't happy, and it's been tearing me apart. You made me feel like such a blind jerk."

"I'm sorry," I whispered.

"I don't know if I'm ready to forgive you yet."

"That's okay."

"And I don't know if I can give you my blessing either. I'm sorry, but if you want to be with Cole, then you need to just get over the fact it'll wound me."

"I can't call him, David. I can't run into his arms if it's gonna hurt you even more. I've done enough damage."

"Don't put this on me, Ella."

Tears lined my lashes as I shook my head. "I don't want to be with him under a cloud. If he finds me, I won't run away, but I'm not coming back to Chicago." I sniffed. "You take care, David. Thanks for hearing me out."

I slashed at my tears and pulled the phone away from my ear, pressing the END button before he could say anything else.

Pulling my knees to my chest, I rested my forehead against them and cried wretched tears that convulsed my body. Nighttime slowly crept over me as I laid my head to the grass, soaking the blades with my tears.

THIRTY-EIGHT
COLE

The bar at Quigg's had never been as shiny as it was now. I'd become a wiping magician. I didn't know why. I guess it felt therapeutic somehow. It was a circular, robotic motion that I could concentrate on. As soon as my mind began to wander, I'd pull it back into place by watching my cloth spin round and round on the counter top.

I'd been living back here for five months now. I worked every spare minute I had and spent the rest of my time in classes or studying. When I was at campus, I kept my head down. I didn't want to talk to anybody, and I sure as hell didn't want to meet any girls.

I knew Nina and Malachi were worried about me, but I just ignored their quiet comments and kept about my business. In a few months' time, school would end, and I could finally put my deposit down on the place I'd found in the south side of town. Malachi had checked it out with me and thought it was a good spot. It needed a shit-load of renovations, but I didn't care; it'd be something to keep me busy over the summer. Nina had sat with me for hours looking at my trust fund and helping me figure out what to spend and where to spend it. They were a little dubious about me going into this venture on my own, but I needed something to pour my energy into.

I couldn't think of Ella. If my mind ever wandered in that direction, it paralyzed me. I ached for her in every way possible. I'd even shed tears, cried into my pillow like some tween girl who'd broken up with her boyfriend. I hated myself for it. I worried about Ella constantly, wondering where she was. I knew she didn't want to leave me. I just knew it. But she had. She'd put her guilt over David above everything else.

I'd worked through the emotions—denial, anger, despair. Nina had talked me through it all. I certainly hadn't reached my higher ground and I felt stuck in the middle of a bog, sinking daily, wondering if I'd ever have the strength to pull myself to the other side. The only thing to get a smile out of me was the prospect of my bar. It'd be hard. I'd have to work like a damn dog, but I could do it.

Throwing my cloth behind the bar, I checked the stock for tonight. Thursday nights were sometimes a little busier, and we didn't want to run out of booze. The door creaked open, and I looked across the room at the lone patron.

My stomach coiled, and I had to force my face not to show it.

Pressing my hands into the polished wood, I

forced a closed-mouth smile. "Hey."

David greeted me with a nod and slipped into the seat in front of me.

"I didn't expect to ever see you walk in here."

"I didn't think I ever would, either." David pursed his lips, struggling to make eye contact with me.

I tapped the bar with my finger, my lips twitching as I struggled for something to say.

"Can I get you a beer?"

"Yeah, please." David nodded and I got to work. He picked up the cardboard coaster and spun it in his hands, dropping it down when I placed the dark ale in front of him.

"It's on the house."

David lifted the glass and nodded his thanks before taking a long swig.

"So, uh, how's life?" I scratched at the counter top, resisting the urge to reach for my cloth and wipe it clean.

"Yeah, not bad. School's school, you know." He shrugged.

"Still maintaining your A+ average?"

"Yep." He pressed his lips together. "It's tiring, but I know I won't regret it. I'm taking the summer off. Paul's invited me to London, so I'm gonna go and check out Europe with my big bro and meet my new nephew."

"Awesome. That'll be great." I smiled, feeling good that he was moving on. I wished I could do the same.

"Yeah, I'm looking forward to it."

David took another long swig of his beer, still not looking at me. It was frickin' torture, and eventually I couldn't help drumming my fingers on the bar. Letting out an awkward chuckle, I looked him square in the face.

"So, are you here to finish me off or forgive me

or...what?"

David smiled, his tongue poking out the edge of his mouth as he tipped his head in consideration. "Not here to finish you off. Not sure I'll ever be able to forgive you, but I just came to say that maybe you were right."

My lips parted.

David's jaw popped to the side. "Ella and I didn't really have that thing. You know, that x-factor people talk about. I didn't think it mattered, but maybe it would have. I mean, I hate to sing, and dancing...no way. I can't stand that song 500 miles or whatever it's called and she loves it. I'd rather go watch a soccer game, and she'd rather sit through *Dirty Dancing* for the fifty-billionth time. I don't know, maybe Ella and I could have lasted the distance, but...did she inspire you? I mean, did she make you deliriously happy? Is she the kind of girl you'd redefine future for?"

I gripped the bar and nodded. "Yeah, man. She was...like no one else." I finished in a whisper.

David paused, finally looking me in the eye. His gaze was reluctant and unsure.

The thick silence was killing me, and I was about to fill it with some sentiment about how it didn't even matter anymore, but he spoke before I could.

"She called me, you know."

My heart stopped. "When?"

"About a month ago."

"Is she okay? Where is she?"

David took a sip of his beer, making me want to throttle him. Answer the damn question!

Unless he didn't know.

I closed my eyes, dropping my head forward. "Let me guess, she wouldn't tell you."

"You're still in love with her, aren't you?" David set his beer down.

"Man, I think I always will be. I wish I could forget her sometimes, but she's just always there." I pointed to my head then slapped my hand against my heart, emotion clogging my throat like it always did.

David nodded, tapping the bar as he stood. He wiped his nose with his finger and sniffed. "I'm sorry I pummeled you that night. Even though I wanted to at the time, I don't think I could've actually killed you. Not because you'd kick my ass before I could, but, well, you were my best friend."

His words sliced through me, making me feel wounded and sore.

"I never meant to..."

"I know." He raised his hand. "We'll never be friends again. I can't do it. But we're cool, okay. It's done." He nodded and walked to the door.

I wanted to call out a thank you, but it felt lame somehow.

He paused at the door, grabbing the handle, but stopped before opening it. "She's at Bellevue College in Washington. That's all I know."

I stopped breathing, unable to speak as he swung the door open and left. My brain froze for a minute, too blown away by what it just heard to even function. Running a shaky hand through my hair, I tried to focus on slowing my heart before it exploded inside my chest.

What did I do now? Go after her?

Did she even want me to?

She left me.

As much as she didn't want to, she actually did, and she hadn't come back either. In fact, she'd done everything in her power to stop me from finding her. Morgan's stubborn lips had remained sealed no matter how hard I'd tried. I'd even tracked down Jody through Facebook and tried to appeal to her, but Ella's friends were loyal.

What would it mean if I did go?

Would I move to Washington, set up a new life with her there? Would we do the long-distance thing?

I squeezed my eyes shut. "Stop getting ahead of yourself, you moron," I muttered.

It really came down to one simple question. Did I want to turn up on Ella's doorstep and risk her rejection on the chance she'd give us one more shot?

Yes.

A smile burst across my face.

I wanted Ella, and all that was left to do now was go and tell her.

The phone in my back pocket buzzed, distracting my planning.

I glanced at the caller ID and nearly didn't answer, but Chaos was playing at Quigg's tomorrow night, and it was probably a last-minute detail thing. "Hey, Jimmy."

"Hey, man, just wondering if we could set up at lunchtime tomorrow and have a little practice at the pub."

"Won't you be at school?"

"Teacher-only day, dude." I could hear the smile in his voice. I grinned along with him then got hit with an insane idea. It was so good, I couldn't ignore it.

My eyes grew wide, and I gripped the phone in my hand.

"So, you're free all day tomorrow?"

"Yep."

A low chuckle resonated in my chest. "I've got a gig for you then."

"Okay, cool. Give me some details. Where is it? What time? How many songs do you want in the set?"

My lips tipped up with a slow smile. "Just one."

THIRTY-NINE

ELLA

It had been a month since I'd called David with my apology. I was really hoping it'd make me feel better, but I was more unsettled than ever. I hadn't meant to make him feel like I needed his blessing, but it must have been playing on my subconscious. It bugged me that it was. Why did I need it? It wasn't my fault I'd fallen in love with Cole and the timing had been super crappy! Why should I have to have David's say-so to pursue it?

I hated that I'd let my need for his approval rule me for so long. It was like a bad habit I couldn't break. I needed to stand up for myself and stop doing that kind of thing.

As I sat through Professor Croft's lecture on the impact of music and movies on tween culture, my mind became more resolute. I wanted Cole, and if I wanted him, then I had to go and get him. Even if he told me I was too late, I had to know.

Professor Croft clapped her hands together. "Okay, so that's it from me today. Make sure you compile a list of all the movies and music you were obsessed with at the age of twelve before you return next week. I'm looking forward to some good discussions."

Books slapped shut and bags were zipped closed. People rose from their places, filing out the door. I slowly gathered my stuff together. I couldn't seem to do anything quickly these days. I was depressed; that was the simple truth. It didn't matter that I was pursuing some of the things I loved. I didn't have the main thing I wanted, so the rest seemed pointless.

I'd run away to figure out what I wanted and now I knew. The only problem was, I was too chicken to go and get it.

Throwing my bag up onto my shoulder, I slipped out the back door and descended the stairs. I could hear a muffled thumping coming from the quad and frowned. I didn't know there was a free concert today.

A girl skipped down the stairs behind me, throwing me an odd glance. "What's that noise?"

"Sounds like a band in the quad." I shrugged.

As we drew closer to the doors, the noise became clearer and I smiled, recognizing the song.

"I Would Walk 500 Miles" by the Proclaimers. It was a goodie.

By the time I reached the bottom of the stairs, I was humming along, but the tune caught in my throat. The girl in front of me pulled the door open and I heard it. It was a rich, perfect sound that shot fire through my veins.

Not just anyone was singing that song.

It was Cole.

I lunged for the door, swinging it open and bursting into the sunlight. A group of students were standing at the top of the stairs, staring at the band. I recognized the good-looking guitarist behind Cole.

Chaos.

He'd brought Chaos all the way from Chicago?

Cole held the microphone, singing with gusto as his eyes scanned the crowd. He was looking for me.

My heart did a double-beat as I stood there watching him.

"Who is that guy?" The girl in front of me pointed.

"Beats me." The student beside her shrugged. "When they were setting up, I heard him say he'd sing the song all day if he had to."

"Why's he singing it?"

"Because he loves me." They both looked at me like I was a total fruitcake.

I smiled and squeezed between them, walking down the steps, my eyes trained on Cole. He spotted me as I reached the pathway leading toward him, his face lighting up like a fireworks display. Jumping down from the stage, he held the microphone tight and walked toward me, singing, "When I'm lonely, oh I know I'm gonna be, I'm gonna be the man who's lonely without you…and when I'm dreamin', oh I know I'm gonna dream, I'm gonna dream about the time when I'm with you."

My grin was so wide, I could feel my cheeks straining.

He kept singing as he closed the gap, and when he reached me, he placed a gentle hand on my face and sang, "And when I come home, yes I'm know I'm gonna be, I'm gonna be the man that comes back home with you. I'm gonna be the man that's coming ho-me to you."

Lowering the microphone, he let the band take over the song as he rubbed his thumb gently over my cheekbone.

"I know you didn't invite me here." He swallowed. "But when David told me where you were, I had to come."

I blinked slowly, not quite believing that everything I wanted was falling into place.

"But I would walk 500 miles and I would walk 500 more..." Jimmy sang.

I chuckled. "And you just had to sing this song, didn't you."

Cole grinned, snatching me to him and lifting me high. My butt rested on his solid forearms as my legs came around his torso. He looked up at me, his eyes gleaming. "You're putty in my hands now, right?"

I brushed my fingers through his curls. "I've been putty in your hands since the first time I heard your luscious voice."

He grinned, looking like a triumphant schoolboy. "I love you, birdy."

"I love you." I leaned toward him for a kiss, but he pulled back, his expression serious. "I have no idea what the future looks like for us, but I'm really keen to work it out...together."

A slow smile spread across my lips. "That's exactly what I want."

Our grins pressed together, the sweet softness of his lips stirring that familiar fire within me. The rest of the world faded around us and we became the only two people in that quad. It was just me, Cole, and the most romantic song I knew.

****

Thank you so much for reading Fever. If you've enjoyed it and would like to show me some support, please consider leaving a review on the site you purchased this book from.

*****

Morgan's story is next in the Songbird Series!

FIGHT FOR YOU is due for release November 2014!! .

ACKNOWLEDGEMENTS

It's always such a pleasure to work on a novel and part of that pleasure comes from working with amazing people.

Thank you so much to:

My critique partners: Cassie & Anna. Your feedback was brilliant. Thank you for making this story stronger.

My editor: Laurie. You are so brilliant to work with. I love your advice and knowledge. Thank you for making my writing better.

My proofreaders: Kristin, Suzy, Karen, Marcia and Lindsey. What would I do without your last-minute catches? Thanks so much, ladies. Your help and enthusiasm means so much to me.

My cover designer: Regina. You are one talented woman and working with you has been such a thrill. Thank you for taking on this project.

My promo designer: Kate. Thank you for your unwavering support and your willingness to drop everything to help me. You are so talented and I love the stuff I always find in my inbox from you.

My publicity team: Mark My Words Publicity. Thank you!!!! You girls are so spectacular. I love working with you. Thank you for helping me launch this book into the world.

My fellow writers: Inklings and Indie Inked. Thank you for always being there to listen and help me. Thank you for sharing your ideas and your own experiences. It's a total honor to be part of your writing journeys.

My readers: As always, thank you. I appreciate you guys so much. Thank you for giving my work a chance. You are turning my dreams into reality.

My friends: A special mention to Nadine and Sharyn...my singing buddies. Thank you for all the laughter, good times and of course...the glorious music.

My family: Thank you to my supportive group of cheerleaders who constantly encourage me to keep pushing, and keep striving to be the best author I can be.

My Prince Charming: Thank you for dancing me into the sunset. I love you.

My savior: Thank you for loving me in spite my faults and giving me the courage to step out of a bad relationship and then letting me meet the perfect man for me.

OTHER BOOKS BY MELISSA PEARL

The Songbird Series

Fight For You (Due for release: Nov 2014)

The Fugitive Series

I Know Lucy - Set Me Free

The Masks Series

True Colors

Two Faced (Releasing: 2014)

Snake Eyes (Releasing: 2014-2015)

Poker Face (Releasing: 2015)

The Time Spirit Trilogy

Golden Blood - Black Blood - Pure Blood

The Betwixt Series

Betwixt - Before - Beyond

The Elements Trilogy

Unknown - Unseen - Unleashed

The Mica & Lexy Series

Forbidden Territory

http://www.melissapearlauthor.com

ABOUT MELISSA PEARL

Melissa Pearl is a kiwi at heart, but currently lives in Suzhou, China with her husband and two sons. She trained as an elementary school teacher, but has always had a passion for writing and finally completed her first manuscript in 2003. She has been writing ever since and the more she learns, the more she loves it.

She writes young adult and new adult fiction in a variety of romance genres - paranormal, fantasy, suspense, and contemporary. Her goal as a writer is to give readers the pleasure of escaping their everyday lives for a while and losing themselves in a journey...one that will make them laugh, cry and swoon.

MELISSA PEARL ONLINE

Website:

melissapearlauthor.com

YouTube Channel:

youtube.com/user/melissapearlauthor

Facebook:

facebook.com/melissapearlauthor

Twitter:

twitter.com/MelissaPearlG

Pinterest:

pinterest.com/melissapearlg/

You can also subscribe to Melissa Pearl's Book
Updates Newsletter. You will be the first to know
about any book news, new releases and giveaways.

http://eepurl.com/p3g8v

CPSIA information can be obtained at www.ICGtesting.com
Printed in the USA
LVOW08s0418131016

508538LV00003BA/185/P